Praise for Mouths of Babes

"[Mouths of Babes] shouldn't just be seen as a great piece of crime writing; it's a fine novel, as good as anything you'll read this year from a 'literary' imprint."
—*Independent on Sunday* (UK)

"Duffy knows how to build suspense and has created an engagingly human heroine." —*The Daily Mail* (UK)

"An unsettling, absor'   ⌐   ⌐ " *The Times* (UK)

"[Mouths of Babes]
novel … Fans will n⌐

"[Mouths of Babes] is a powerful novel about teenage angst and playground power, our innermost secrets, the treachery of bullying and the dishonesty that can lie at the heart of the closest relationships … Duffy proves yet again what a skilled writ⌐⌐ ⌐h⌐ i⌐ " *The Pink Paper*

"Fast-paced, candi⌐
ten an intelligent t⌐
of human behavio⌐

"*Mouths of Babes*

MOUTHS OF BABES

STELLA DUFFY

BLOODY BRITS PRESS

Ann Arbor and Alnmouth

2008

7-08
15-

Bloody Brits Press
PO Box 3671
Ann Arbor MI 48106-3671

Printed in the United States of America on acid-free paper.

BLOODY BRITS PRESS FIRST EDITION
First Printing April 2008

Bloody Brits Press is an imprint of Bywater Books

This book was first published in Great Britan by
Serpent's Tail in 2005.

Cover designer: Bonnie Liss (Phoenix Graphics)

ISBN 978-1-932859-53-9

for Eli and Lucille

Thanks to Pete Ayrton, Stephanie Cabot, Shelley Silas, Rebecca Armstrong, Mark Billingham, John Williams, Ruthie Petrie, Wilf, The Broody Board, and the Thelma and Louise of road trip reading— Val McDermid and Lauren Henderson.

ONE

You all watched it happen. It happened to me, but it also happened to you. We were there at the same time. Each of you said you'd seen it, witnessed the exact same event. But I was there too, and my point of view was different to yours. Your backs were to the wall—mine wasn't. I saw it all. You only saw me. And from where I was standing I could see all of you, each of you, quite clearly.

And though you said they were, your stories were not the same.

TWO

Molly lay in bed. She'd already turned off the radio alarm three times, was reaching out her hand to turn it off again. A bomb somewhere. An earthquake somewhere else. An old dead movie star, another royal idiocy, a major scientific breakthrough promised. Maybe. Next year. Or the year after. If the funding comes through. Constantly waiting for funding. All of it utterly banal, pointless, as relevant as the weather. Squally showers to start, growing fine in the east, cooler tonight. She turned onto her side and stared at the new-bought clothes hanging on the wardrobe, darker and less distinct through the shadowed morning light. Molly had only bought these clothes yesterday, a whole new outfit. Too much money and an uncaring pin number offered up on her credit card. Uncaring, not caring, don't care, can't care, care too much.

But now the clothes seemed unreal, in the shop still, on a mannequin. Not for her body, hers to wear. Surely it couldn't be right to wear them. But she would wear them, just the once. Wear them out, out on the street, into the car and to the places she had no choice but to go, her day carefully planned and moving ahead whether she liked it or not. Long white skirt, fitted white jacket. Both lined in robin red silk to match the dark red choli. New bra, new knickers. Red again. Silk again. Shoes sitting below the ensemble. Red shoes. Sexy shoes, high heels, red leather. Not funeral shoes. That was the point, her point. Molly didn't want to be dressing for a funeral, this funeral. She didn't want to be dressing at all, ever again. Didn't want to be putting on the clothes, giving in to the light behind the curtains, making it real. Every day that turned into sleep-free night and another shattered morning made it more real, took her further from then, the time before this. The time before now.

Not funeral shoes. Not funeral clothes, not strictly, white for mourning but the red too red, too statement. Fuck it. Wearing them anyway. Molly turned off the radio alarm, the moaning droning voices, and closed her eyes again, trying to find sleep, a place of safety; place of not-this, not-here, not-now. Trying to force herself back into a space where she wasn't getting up for the funeral, where she wasn't dressing up against her will for an event she couldn't bear was happening, would happen, had to happen. Booked and paid for and planned and agreed and all nicely arranged to within five minutes of get-me-to-the-cemetery-on-time. Busy cemetery, bodies lining up, the living queuing up with their lying-down dead, careful not to miss their allocated slot, not to spill their own grief over those leaving before, the others waiting after. The funeral director had been very specific, honest, a plain language specialist Molly might have appreciated in another time, not this time. This particular cemetery was a very busy place. They had their hour booked. Molly had to get out of bed. Today was the day.

She wasn't going to cry again. Not now, not yet, not before she'd even lifted her head from the pillow, while the curtains were still closed, the street outside quiet. For the past week she'd finally gone to bed around midnight, woken at three, four at the latest, and waited crying in the dark for another day to happen. Another day that would bring sympathy cards in the post and too many flowers for the small front room and phone calls she couldn't bring herself to answer. But she would. Molly was good like that. Polite. Well brought up. Getting up.

In the shower she knew she was washing her skin, her long black hair, shampoo and conditioner, shaving brown legs, concave armpits, making herself nice. And good. Good girl. Razor reaching for scalp. She could shave her head too. Make a statement, harsher than the shoes, show on the outside what was going on inside. Bare, bared, unbearable. Except that it was. Anything was, everything was. Bearable, do-able, carry-on-able. Molly knew that now. Had guessed it before, seen it on the faces of the parents she dealt with daily at the hospital, grief-stricken at their own child's pain, or even their own child's death, and yet, astonishingly, still breathing.

3

But she really knew it now—the planet demands we keep turning with it—and, incredibly, we do. The water was turning cold, must have forgotten to put it on overnight again, she didn't care much. Hot, cold. Whatever. Washing felt utterly unnecessary. Had done since that first phone call six days ago, disembodied voice speaking aloud and making no sense. All of it meaningless and yet so incredibly ordinary at the same time, normal activities turned stupid ever since. Stupid and hard, hands moving through quicksand to make a cup of tea she couldn't drink, milk turning sour in her hand, mouth forming impossible shapes to say the impossible words, taxis and buses and cars and bicycles, all with everyone carrying on, still breathing. Except the one Molly wanted breathing. Lying down, laid out, cold.

Molly remembered a story her grandmother had told her, passed down through generations of early-widowed women, about an aunt who followed the old ways. Suttee had long been outlawed, and this aunt had been desperate to throw herself on the husband's funeral pyre, plenty of older women ready to help her, but various authorities at the funeral, standing around to make sure it wouldn't be done, taking care to prove that their village was as modern and enlightened as the next. The aunt was finally dragged from the cold ashes and taken home, where she sat still, refusing to eat or speak. Refused to wash for forty days. There was nothing they could do, short of pushing the old woman into a bath. They could keep her alive but they couldn't keep her clean.

Molly liked the idea. Greasy hair and filthy clothes, unwashed mouth, ragged fingernails. She wanted the outer show, the proof of mourning. Remembered the white suit and the red shoes, everything depending on her clothes, and nearly smiled. Sunshine through the bathroom window. Proof of morning. She rinsed her clean hair in cold water, turned off the taps, dried her shivering skin. Applied deodorant, moisturizer, body cream, perfume. Performed the actions. The ones she had also performed for the cold body. Combed and dried her hair, long and straight and black. Pulled it back tight, hard as she could, hard as her mother had when she was a little girl and first wearing the long, long plaits to school. Stood naked in front of the mirror and didn't know why it was she was still standing. Dressed anyway. Was ready and waiting for when they would come to get her, join her, hold her hand as they all went off together. The standing ones, still-breathing ones, and the cold waxy dead one in the pale narrow box.

Molly had been ready for almost an hour, sitting, not moving, when finally a key turned in the front door, there were footsteps, someone called her name, a quiet voice, uncertain, and then Saz stood there, their baby daughter sleepy in her arms.

"Moll? Are you ready?"

"No."

"You look ready. You're dressed. That's good."

"I don't want to go."

"You look lovely. The suit looks lovely."

"Shoes?"

"The shoes are perfect, babe."

"Sure?"

"Perfect. He'd have loved them, the gesture."

"I can't come. Not yet."

Saz shifted the waking baby girl to her other hip. "Right, OK. Well, what else do you need? Bag? Tissues?"

Molly pointed to the bag at her feet. "I've got it all. I did everything you said."

"Good. That's good. So we should go now. Babe?"

"I can't." Molly shook her head, more tears, falling unnoticed, important. "I can't do this."

Saz's voice even quieter now, Matilda wriggling in her arms, grizzling to be put down, she blew a distracted kiss across their fractious daughter's curls, held out her free hand to Molly. "We really do have to go. Your mum's waiting in the car, she doesn't want to come inside."

"She doesn't like being here. Without him. It doesn't feel like their house." Molly shook her head. "But I think it does. I think if we just ignore all this it will be as if he hasn't gone. We can just leave it as it is. His things," she stroked the week-old newspaper, unfinished crossword clues stretched out across the top of the page, "we can just leave it. Like he only went out to the shop or something. This is mad. He was here and now he's not."

5

"Yeah. It is." Saz looked at the old wooden clock on the mantel-piece. "Come on, babe, we have to go. Your mum needs you with her, we both do. We picked up your uncle, he said the flight was all right, but he really doesn't look OK."

"I'm not OK."

"Of course you're not. None of you are. You don't have to be."

"But they all want me to act as if it's fine, as if this is normal."

"Dying is normal, sweetie. And they don't care how you behave, they just want you with them, sitting with them."

Molly ran her fingers over the newspaper again, picking out incomplete words, looking for signs, finding nothing.

"I want my dad."

"I know you do."

THREE

Three boys, two girls. Boys and girls here, now, though in another time and place they would clearly be men and women. Tall enough, broad enough, shapely enough. Ready. They were standing around her. In a tight little playground circle. Only this wasn't playing. Looked like talking, gossiping, sharing secrets. But it wasn't that either. There was laughter and something that sounded like singing. Or maybe wailing. On closer inspection it was a humming behind clenched teeth that an open mouth would turn into wailing. An open mouth would turn into words not to be spoken, words too dangerous to let out. She would not open her mouth, she knew better than that. And there would be no closer inspection either. No one was coming close, they never did. These kids were scary. Scary to the other kids and, truth be told—though it never was—scary to the teachers too. Not violent scary, obvious, brutal—nothing as uncouth as that, these kids were interesting scary, clever scary, cool. Their five person grouping of arty and weird and choosing-to-be different that made walking past them that little bit more frightening. Whispered giggling, snide remarks, always the possibility of something more, a scent of danger. Once there were keys scratched along car doors in the staff carpark, never in the open, never anything anyone could prove, and even if it had been, this group would have been horrified at the suggestion that one of their number might have used anything as prosaic as a bunch of keys for their vandal's tool. They liked razor blades—on skin as well as things it was rumored. Preferred weird American music with Japanese influences, black and white films you had to read as well as watch. The fear was in the possibility of bumping into this lot on the street, in the reinforced concrete, imitation High Street shopping precinct where they roamed their Saturdays, looking for anything that might take them away from the normal they so despised. Walkways built for baby buggies and slow old people, reclaimed for skateboards and bikes and swathes of youth. Coming across these kids, out of school, a gang of them and just one of you, kids freed from the restraining armor of uniform, teachers exposed by the lack of books and boards—that was what scared the adults. So the teachers knew some of what went on and yet they said nothing. The knowledge was there, on both sides. In your eyes. In their looks. In the sideways, smirking, fuck-you looks. They were good, these kids. Really good at bad.

She had stupidly come round to their part of the school playground. The place they had made their own. She knew better, but somehow, not really thinking, she'd gone there anyway. And he'd called her up, the good-looking one, oldest one, Will Gallagher. And she'd been scared to say no, so she came at his bidding. Had hardly ever been up here before, the raised section of the courtyard. It was just the crappiest, least sunny corner of an old-fashioned playground really, only some ex-Headmaster had died and left a bunch of money, and the Board of Governors thought it might be a nice gesture to have the whole area redone. It was meant to be a privilege to hang out down this end. That was the lecture they were given at the beginning of term anyway—they weren't kids anymore, though not quite the oldest in the school, so they didn't get a lounge to themselves, but they were big enough to be responsible, to not need to be directly under the staffroom windows, like the younger ones in the main playground. Big enough to not need supervised breaks, to be trusted in this raised corner, hidden corner. First there was a slightly elevated section with some wooden tables and benches, then a short flight of concrete stairs up to a crappy little rock garden, and then another half dozen stairs up again to where the concrete leveled out. The plants had grown well since it was originally laid out when they were just first-years, heavy flaxes had taken good root in the dry, sandy soil and now it was the perfect spot, right in the corner and at the top, with a ten-foot drop back down to the ground. Daniel Carver had jumped it once. Sprained his ankle really fucking badly. Of course Will had made the jump safely a couple of times already, but then he was fitter and better at that sort of thing. Anyway, after the skinny, lanky Daniel sprained his ankle, the caretaker built up this little three-foot wall. As if that would stop guys jumping down when they were showing off. It didn't. But the fact that Will Gallagher's little group made it their special place effectively stopped anyone else going there at all. It was a perfect vantage point. See without being seen. Just the way they liked it.

Anyway, Will had called her up and because she was stupid and scared she'd come and now they were standing around her, the girl. Third time this month. And it was only the thirteenth. Unlucky again.

"Fucking lezz."

"Dirty dyke bitch."

"Do you like it?"

"Is that what you like? Like that?"

Whispered words, always whispered, creeping into her ears and staying there, festering, making her sick.

A hand crosses a breast, stops, not long enough to say it was meant, not brief enough to pretend it wasn't. No tears yet. She's holding onto the tears, knows what her crying does to them, red rags to bulls, furious goring bulls spinning round to beat up on inept goading baby-boy matadors. She is no fighter. Even if she was, there's never anyone on her side when something like this happens. Of course she has friends, officially, sort of. Two of the girls in her year, one guy, not many, no real group of her own. The few kids she's sort of friends with now are like her—too clever, too stupid, too rich, too poor, too much—they are the easy prey, and long gone round the gray corners, into the hollow buildings with their smell of teenage sweat and cleaning fluids and caged frustration. No one stupid enough to get in the way, make themselves the next target. Not when this target is always so pathetically ready. She knows she does it to herself, knows she is an idiot. Why did she come into school early today? She should have waited as she had done for the past ten days, waited at the corner of her own street and made the final run for it, run the risk of being late, a detention carrying far more pleasure than pain. Kept in an hour after school, by the time she was allowed to leave they'd all be off, doing whatever it was they did when they got together at someone's house, one of their houses, then she would be able to get home safely as well. In late, out late. The detention was always worth it. Except her dad had a go last time, the last time she'd brought home a detention slip for him to sign. Your daughter arrived late yet again. Getting to be a problem. Parental responsibility, parental necessity. Said he'd bloody well drop her off at school himself if she couldn't get there, said he'd march her up to the gates. And then where would she be? All of them seeing her father bring her in, Daddy walking her up to the gates and handing her over for the group sacrifice, sitting target with still more ammunition for the circle.

So she'd come in early today instead, hoping to make a run for it, hide out in the library maybe, place of safety for all the misfits, but they'd caught her, seen her from their viewing platform and called her up there, and she wasn't brave enough to just walk on, risk their wrath by ignoring them. Will Gallagher started it, he always started it. Not that the others took a whole lot of encouraging. He was starting it again.

"Time you and I had a little chat."

There is nothing to chat about. Nothing to say. She feels sick. Tighter circle, the smell of their breath now. Toothpaste and cigarettes and cheese and onion crisps bought from the shop on the corner. (Two Schoolchildren At One Time ONLY.) She can't quite see above them, she's not that tall, not as tall as Will or Daniel. She can see the edge of the Science Block roof, the sloping gutter, tops of the highest windows, and that's it. And them. She can see them. Another hand on her shoulder, her lower back, her bum. Her bum cheek. Holds it, gone. She turns around and it's gone.

"What?"

"Nothing."

"No, what? Why did you turn round?"

"I didn't."

"Liar."

"I didn't ..."

"Fucking liar!"

"No, I just thought ..."

"You thought we turned? We turned round maybe? Quick one-eighty you didn't even notice? We turned round and you stayed in the same place. Is that it?"

"Um, yeah ... maybe. I don't know."

"Jesus, you're more stupid than you look. Have the buildings moved, stupid girl?"

Nothing, she can say nothing. But nothing is not good enough. Just let the bell ring. Please let it ring. When the bell rings it will get better, she can go into her class and even Andrea Browne, the one of them that's in French with her, won't be so bad. Not by herself, there's always a chance Andrea will say something really bitchy, always, but when she's by herself she'll usually drop it for the hour of the class at least. The others don't seem to know it, but when Andrea Browne is by herself she changes, she's quieter, tries harder. It's like there's two of her—one who's sharp and mean and funny with it, who never seems to work and yet does really well anyway, then the other Andrea Browne who gets on with things and is quiet and really wants to pass her exams and go to university and get the fuck out of here. The Andrea Browne who once said all she wanted was an easy job and a nice bloke and some nice kids. And then looked around, stunned that she'd said it out loud, glared at the girl just for hearing her. But Andrea never shows that side of herself round this lot. This lot, round the girl. Round and round.

"Well ... why ... did ... you ... turn ... round?"

She has to answer now. Sneaks a look at the watch on the wrist of a tight fist. Five minutes too long. She has to answer.

"I thought he ... he touched me."

"Me?"

Spun around again. Face to face. The lanky one, brightest one, Daniel, still has spots, she can smell the Clearasil, close enough to smell the Clearasil.

"Touched you? I touched you? Where?"

"Nowhere. Nothing. It doesn't matter."

"Oh, but it absolutely fucking does."

He won't let it go. They are all so close, she's really hot, she knows she's sweating. Made her mum buy a really expensive deodorant at Boots last weekend, told her she just had to. She's praying it works. But the smell of her fear is rising, acid and damp. Maybe it will rain, there are clouds up above. In the section of the world she can see, separated heads, far enough apart to see clouds. Maybe it will rain, they will go inside, the girls won't want the rain to spoil their hair. Maybe it will rain. Not yet.

"He said, touched you where?"

Has to say something. "On ... on my shoulder."

"Oh. Right. Like this?"

Shove. A light enough shove, but she's pushed into Will's chest. Three boys, two girls. Except that Will Gallagher is a man-boy. He smiles as he stands her up, helps her regain her balance, hands on her upper arms that might be kind. Might be. She almost smiles back, there is a crease at the corner of her mouth but she holds it back, scared it will turn to a yell, to tears. His girlfriend Andrea catches it.

"Excuse me! Are you smiling at my boyfriend, you fucking lezzie cunt?"

The second girl giggles, it sounds funny in Andrea's posher voice, the one Andrea speaks in when her mother's around, the one she usually drops for school. Cunt. Fucking lezzie cunt. Second girl adds in, "You think Daniel actually wants to touch you?"

"No. Of course not. I ... wouldn't. I didn't ... I ..."

And then tears, she can't stop them. Tears like she's weeing herself in the Juniors, hot and yellow down her legs. Tears like she has no control. She has no control.

And Daniel Carver's still asking, politely, carefully. "Tell me. Where do you think I touched you?"

Tears.

"Where do you think I touched you? Say it." More tears. Pissing down her face.

"Say it. Say it. Say it."

A quiet chant, utterly insistent. Impossible to deny. "On my back. My lower back."

"Where?"

"My … my bum. I thought he touched my bum."

Silence then. They move back. Light comes in from above their heads. The biology lab, chemistry room. Mrs. Chester's maths class. Daniel, the clever one with spots, looks down at her, no smile from Will now either, not even pretending humor, not even so he can show his beautiful smile. They are all five disgusted, horrified.

"On your bum? Oh my God. That is so gross. My hand accidentally touched your bum. I feel sick. I feel so fucking sick. Quick somebody, cut my fucking hand off. Her bum. I touched her bum. Her bottom. Her arse. Oh God. I touched a lesbian bottom. I'm probably going to die."

Daniel moves off, down the stairs, hand held out in front of him, he's loud now, this is for the whole school, for them all. Big theatrics, lots of laughter, applause even, some laughing too from the edges of the asphalt, from the happy ones, those she has saved from torment by her presence. By her sacrifice.

Will Gallagher follows, Andrea runs after, and then the other two. They are giggling among themselves. For Andrea Browne there is joy, she is in love, she and Will reinforced, there is union in the joint action. Later in the evening she will work hard at her homework, the good girl side of her will out. For now she is just excited to have let out her wild again. The wild she craves and fears. For Daniel it has been an achievement, lead bastard, not usually his role. He likes it, hopes Will has noted it—hopes Andrea did as well. For Will it has been another scenario, swiftly accomplished, though it's true he prefers to be the center of attention himself, doesn't mind Daniel coming up with good ideas, as long as he can act them out. Still, next time. He walks away singing to himself. A French song, one he learned to impress Andrea. One he learned to impress himself. To Ewan, the youngest of the three boys, there is satisfaction at the quick five-minute break from routine, and a hope that he too looked as cool as the others, was as cool as them. For Sally the feeling is something else altogether. Relief. Relief it wasn't her. Relief that she is with them, part of this group, safe in this group. Because when they are together they are all safe. They might be different to the rest of the school, apart, odd even, but when they are together they are beautiful and shining and funny and clever. And, when she is with them, she is like the others and that makes her beautiful and shining and funny and clever too.

No one looks behind. No one worries about the girl left half-hidden in the corner at the top of the concrete stairs, pissing tears down her crumpled face.

FOUR

Molly's father's sudden death had devastated them both. With a new baby, Saz and Molly had found their own parents' support invaluable—telephone succor, free and readily available with none of the health-visitor panics that cause waking nightmares in the sleep-free nights of new parents. Ian and Asmita were too far away in Scotland to visit often and her mother's Hindi lullaby crooned into the handset didn't hush Matilda's wailing in the slightest, but it calmed Molly anyway. Molly's father on the other end of the phone, finally getting the chance to tell his daughter the truth. Yes, four-week-old babies are very scary. You were. And annoying. And sometimes horrible. You were. And beautiful. This too would pass. Though hopefully Matilda would stay beautiful. You did.

Molly and Saz had both noticed the change in their relationships with their own parents, and with other parents. Friends with children talked to them differently, their mothers treated them differently, they were in the club now, part of the sorority of graduate-women. Proper grownups. And of course they weren't. They were ordinary Saz and Molly with their same old dreams and desires and, once the first few days' endorphin rush had worn off, they were also tired and besotted and irritable and in love with Matilda and wanting their lives back and never wanting to be without Matilda. Ever. (Or maybe just one night. One perfect night of uninterrupted sleep.)

Saz and Molly understood their own parents in a way they never had before. Understood the unbearable, unspeakable truths of bringing home a new person, their new person. Unconditional love inextricably linked with "What the hell have we done?" Something they had suspected when checking out the double-edged admissions of already-parenting friends, but had to feel themselves to truly know it. It was like the grieving; before Ian's death, Molly had imagined she understood what grief felt like. Now she knew.

In the same way that Molly and Saz were living some sort of ground-breaking lives as lesbian mothers, Molly's parents had led a similarly ground-breaking life when they married and, despite the concerns of both families, went on to create their mixed-race daughter. Molly knew this, and Ian and Asmita knew this, and all three were settling in to a more profound understanding of each other than before, parents and children re-connecting as adults, useful to each other, and happy to be so. Then Ian failed to wake up one morning, his heart skipped its beat in the night. Not an old heart, he was only sixty-three. Not an unwell heart, just one of those things, as banal and ghastly as they always are.

Saz understood that her grief was different to Molly's. It was also heavily mixed with guilt. Saz was profoundly aware that while she had an older sister, three nieces and a nephew, and both parents, Molly now had only her mother. As she explained to her old friend and ex-lover Carrie, Matilda burbling beside them in the late summer shade, "It's just always there, seeing Molly in pain. No matter what a good time we're having, or how much Matilda's making us laugh …"

"How much you're laughing at her, you mean."

"Well, yeah, that's what babies are for."

"Like puppies?"

"But better at going to the shop for you when they get older. No, there's this permanent feeling of sadness."

"That's normal, isn't it? They were very close."

"Yeah, but—and I know this is selfish—I'd just planned this perfect first year. All the cute baby stuff, everyone being nice to us, making a fuss … I thought I'd be able to ease into it all, the whole happy families thing."

"And now you have to worry about Molly too?"

Saz shrugged, "Not quite like that, just … well … yes."

"You're right. It does sound selfish. Maybe you need something to distract you?"

"Like what?"

16

"I don't know, I just didn't think you'd be happy not working."

"I didn't know what it would be like."

"But you like it?"

"Weirdly, yes. You know, like now, with Molly getting ready to go back to the hospital, and just me and Matilda at home, I'm loving it. She is a lot of work and I did think I might be bored, but I'm not."

Carrie frowned, "Never? I mean she's gorgeous, of course, but never?"

Saz handed her daughter another noisy plastic piece of primary color to play with, noted Matilda's drooping eyelids with pleasure. "Maybe every now and then," she said. "I am surprised I've found her so entertaining, it's not what I'd expected. But no, not really bored, not yet. There's been all the stuff to do with Ian, none of that has been routine. I haven't been at home by myself with her all that much, people keep visiting, like you now. I just quite like it, playing wife-and-mother."

Carrie poured the last of the wine into their glasses, fished in the bag for crisp crumbs. She still didn't look convinced. "Maybe you're scared?"

"Of what?"

"Your work not turning out the way you'd hoped? The western world is littered with women who had great plans for their working wonders and then, when the whole brilliant career thing doesn't turn out the way they hoped, they give up and have a bunch of kids and hope no one notices."

Saz laughed, "Maybe that's true for women with proper jobs, but I hardly think my freelance work over the past years counts as a 'career.'"

"Why not?"

"Well, there's the fact that I've been relying on Molly for the bulk of our money anyway, and that I still get more than half my income from boring find-my-cheating-lover jobs ..."

Carrie agreed, "OK, when you put it like that. And your last job wasn't exactly a major success."

"Thanks."

"You were in hospital for half Molly's pregnancy."

17

"Ten weeks of the just over nine months. You've always been crap at maths, haven't you?"

"Whatever, you were very sick, Saz."

Saz turned away to concentrate on Matilda. "I know."

"We were scared for you."

"I know."

"It was shit for Molly."

Saz looked at the dark blue sky, at her daughter, at the lawn that needed mowing, the macrocarpa hedge that needed cutting, anywhere but at Carrie. "Yes, Carrie. I know."

"And the rest of us, of course, but so horrible for her while she was pregnant. She was nicer to me then than ever before. Or since."

"Moll's always nice to you."

Carrie picked the chipped pink polish on her big toenail. "No, Saz, Molly's mostly polite to me. Not quite the same. But fair enough that she was worried, it's not the first time you've had a job that ended in disaster."

"Hang on, I've had my successes. It's just that the disasters have been …"

"More spectacular?"

"More painful. And I don't need reminding, I'm the one with the scars."

Carrie licked her fingers clean of grease and salt and lifted the hem of Saz's thin cotton skirt.

"Oi!"

"Just checking. Your scars are pretty good though."

"Helps having a doctor for a wife."

"You can barely tell there was any problem with your hands. And this thigh's all right."

"Carrie, get your hand off my leg." Carrie moved away a little. "The other one's still a bit lumpier though."

"Oh go on, show me? For old times' sake?"

"No!"

Carrie lay back on the grass. "Anyway, the last mess would've put anyone off. You're bloody lucky you came out of that with no scars."

18

Saz massaged her neck, this conversation—as with any that touched on her past damage—causing her muscles to tense, her shoulders to ride up. "Not on the outside. Funny really, my burn scars are always here, like a constant show, and yet that's something I got myself into. Whereas the scars I got from being beaten up—the internal damage, emotional stuff—none of that shows on the outside."

Carrie frowned, "And the funny part about that is what?"

"That the fire—a thing—damaged me, so you can still see it."

"Only if I lift up your skirt."

Saz ignored the grin, checked on her now-sleeping daughter, lowered her voice, "And I'd rather you didn't. Whereas the physical damage from the beating was mostly on the inside and that's all healed now anyway, but the emotional stuff is always going to be there. Scars you can't see."

"Like the scars I have from our relationship?"

"Fuck off, Carrie, you left me. I'm trying to make an important philosophical point."

Carrie stretched out in the late season sun, "I so care."

"Well, you should. Move the umbrella a bit?" Carrie shifted the shade so it more completely covered Matilda's body, and Saz continued, "Now that you're a godmother you should take these things more seriously."

"Umbrellas?"

"The damage people inflict as opposed to things, and yet it's things—fire, water, guns, cars—that we're usually scared of."

"And we should really be scared of people? That's the life-affirming message you want me to teach your daughter?"

"Of course not. Or maybe. I don't know. It's just something I've been thinking about."

"In your long boring days at home all alone with Tilly?"

"Matilda."

"Mattie?"

"Matilda."

"Just wait until she goes to school."

"I will, thank you. And my days are not boring."

"Clearly not, you don't even have the time to put your empties in the recycling bin." Carrie pointed to the four drained wine bottles sitting by the back doorstep.

"Basement flat people always get there first and fill it with theirs. I think we're a bit fed up with having neighbors."

"They're probably fed up with having a screaming baby in the middle of the night."

"She doesn't scream. Never has. Not once. Matilda is an angel."

"Yeah, and you're a liar."

"Well, she's very lovely when she's asleep."

"True, but you don't even have a tiny hankering to take on some new work?"

"No, not yet. When Molly goes back to the hospital, I'll be prime carer. That's plenty for now."

"She'd never let you work now anyway, she's so bloody careful of you, always has been, it's why she's so snippy with me. Scared I might hurt you again. Or worse ..." Carrie pouted ... "not hurt you?"

Saz laughed. "God, Carrie, I might just need more than five hours sleep a night for your suggestive leer to excite anything in me ever again."

"Right. So you're still not shagging?"

"Piss off. It's none of your business. And anyway, Moll's grieving, it's been incredibly hard for her. For me too."

"Of course it has. Her father's dead, she had a bloody hard time with you being hurt, now she wants to share her baby with some- one who's not here any more. It's fucking horrible." Carrie knelt, picked up her bag, planted a careful kiss on Matilda's head and a less gentle one on Saz's lips, "And you're still not shagging."

"We are!"

Carrie just looked. And grinned.

Saz corrected herself, "Occasionally."

"Yes, darling, you join in the new parents' chorus and I'll rush off home. Because while I may not have the ideal must-have accessory for a lesbian about town ..."

"What's that?"

"A baby, Saz."

"Cynic. That is no way to talk about your beloved goddaughter."

"Guard-daughter. Don't do God. Anyway, I may be baby-free, but I am at least getting a shag with fine regularity. So I'll just go home and get my share. And maybe yours while I'm at it."

Carrie left without divulging any further details of her latest conquest—"at least until I see if it's going to last the week"—and Saz moved inside. Baby food, bath, lullabies, and cup of tea. Perfectly content.

FIVE

When the fall happened, when the last push allowed the fall to happen, I wasn't able to speak then. Couldn't say a word. I didn't know who I could tell anyway. Who'd believe me?

But now those words want to be spoken, they are ready to be heard—and I'm ready to let them out. I'm so ready.

Are you?

SIX

Four months after the funeral, Molly was nearing the end of her maternity leave, happy to be at home with Saz and Matilda, excited by their changing life, and growing into who she might be as a mother. And every now and then she was wrenched back to a place where Asmita packed picnic baskets and Ian skipped a shift so they could take the pre-school Molly out for lunch and silly songs by the river. Picnic treats and river songs she wanted to offer her own daughter in time but wasn't sure she knew the recipe, songs she wanted to teach Matilda, songs she was scared she didn't know all the words for and now could never ask. Every good picture, welcome picture, intercut with Ian lying waxy in the coffin.

Another month and Molly went back to work. Three days a week at first, building to full time after a fortnight. On the first day she cried all the way to the hospital, cared for other people's children, soothed panicking parents, and felt like the worst mother in the world. She rushed home and was appalled that Matilda hadn't seemed to notice her absence. Talking to the others at work she found they all felt the same. And not just the mothers. The fathers, the carers, the brothers and sisters, lovers and alone, everyone walking around with a head full of the problems of work, and simultaneously eaten up with the possibilities of home. All these people, in love, grieving, worrying over unpaid bills, dreaming of holidays to come—it was astonishing they could function at all, let alone behave as if they actually deserved the status the white coat and blue uniforms seemed to allow them. And yet they all did. Molly would too.

Molly went to visit Asmita on the last of her long weekends before starting full time, to be with her mother, and to scatter the ashes of her father. Just the two of them, at Asmita's request. And while Molly wanted Saz with her for support, Saz thought she understood Asmita's reasoning.

"Come on, I'll make you coffee."

"Piss off, if it's going to be a lecture I'll have wine, thanks." They walked into the kitchen, Saz leading, pulling her partner on, Molly's arms around Saz's waist, one foot, two foot, forward. Saz poured the wine, emptied a bag of tortilla chips into a bowl, pulled the remains of a tub of hummus from the back of the fridge.

"Is this all right?"

"I don't know. Maybe. Sniff it."

Saz did. "It'll do."

They ate and drank and then Saz went on, "Perhaps having all of us there just rubs it in for your ma, we spend the day together, visit their friends, and then the three of us go to bed, and Asmita has to go to her bedroom alone. There is a chance we make her feel worse as well as better."

Molly drank down half her glass of wine, poured more. "Oh God, I hadn't thought of that."

"You don't have to. You're dealing with your own feelings. But it's bad for her too, maybe worse for her." Molly was quiet then, holding her glass, swirling the deep red liquid, Saz scared she'd said too much. "Babe? I'm sorry, I ..."

"No. I'm sure you're right, of course it's harder for her."

"Well, it's different anyway. And it might be really good for the two of you to have some time to yourselves."

"Maybe, but I'm not sure I even know how to be with her by myself. Dad was always there. I know he told her everything, but I mostly told him first. He was my mate."

Saz thought of her own parents, the constant presence since their retirement of one with the other, how much of her experience with both parents was mediated through her older sister Cassie. "I suppose it's like a new relationship between you and Asmita. I'm sorry it's so hard, Moll."

"Me too. Is there another bottle?"

Saz looked at the clock; they'd had a busy day with visiting dads and a long walk in the park, Matilda's afternoon sleep had been sketchy at best. If they were lucky and her current pattern held fast for another night she would give them a good solid break until six or even seven the next morning. "Yeah. There is."

A while later they got up from the kitchen table, not a little drunk, Molly resolved to make every effort with her mother, allow Asmita to have her own grief, allow herself her own grief. She was easier now, calmed after a good ten minutes alternating laughter and shock at Saz's new story about Carrie's latest non-monogamous girlfriend and a minor celebrity from *Eastenders*. At the door Saz pulled Molly back and they kissed against the wall, kissed with eager mouths and ready hands and twisting legs. Kissed, bodies pressed tight together, pushing out the pain and tiredness and letting in some of the desire that the difficulties of the last few months had kept at bay. Saz's hands inside Molly's clothes, fingers on skin, blood pulsing faster, eager mouths pushing and biting. Then Matilda began to wail from her boxroom at the end of the hall and Saz burst out laughing. "That child has perfect timing."

When Matilda was pacified and they were standing beside her cot in the tiny room, Saz whispered, "What do you think when you look at her?"

Molly shook her head. "Everything. How I want to protect her, how I never want her to get bullied for her skin color or her gay mothers or because she has sticky-out ears."

"She doesn't have sticky-out ears."

"Not yet, who knows what she'll look like in six months' time? But you know what I mean. I got such a hard time when I was little, being the only brown kid where we lived. I never want that for her."

"She'll get a hard time for some reason. Everyone does."

"I know. I just want to save her from it."

"Me too."

"And I feel guilty that I'm not here with her all the time."

"Really?"

"Yeah, often. But I'm also really proud to be providing for you and her, taking care. I still find it incredible that she came from us. I take it for granted for a day or so and then catch myself looking at her and realize all over again how amazing it is, that we really did make her together."

"With Chris."

"Sure, the three of us. Fifteen years ago that would have been unheard of. All those statistics and failures and it might never have worked."

"It mostly doesn't."

"Exactly. But it did for us. We got what we wanted."

"We're lucky."

"Sometimes."

Quiet then, the sound of Matilda in her cot, the soft regular in and out of her sleeping breath, they left the room, walked down the dark hall, arms round each other.

"I love you, Moll."

"That's good."

"But it doesn't make it better, does it?"

"No, it doesn't."

Saz fell asleep after Molly. Carrie was right, they weren't having sex. Not much anyway. Baby tiredness combined with grief-exhaustion had made it hard, sleep the easier option once they were close to their sheets. But she didn't know that it mattered really, maybe later, maybe after a while. For now there was Matilda snuffling in her room down the hall and Molly's warm naked body beside her and Saz was aware of how precarious the balance was. Hugely grateful she had her perfect little family, a small thing like a spasmodic sex life was the last thing she intended to worry about, not yet, anyway. Besides that, she was fairly fucking knackered herself.

SEVEN

Of course it wasn't just her they picked on, that easy-girl, their victim-girl. It never was simply a case of finding an outsider to harass. There were always internecine cracks as well, in-group pain. Daniel once told Will he thought it was how they knew they were a group that really worked, because they checked out their tactics from the inside first. This was after they'd spent the evening mocking Sally for some stupid thing she'd said, some late-night German movie she hadn't understood. Sally didn't always get the things the guys were into, neither did Andrea, but Andrea wasn't stupid enough to say so. Nor was Sally a second time.

Sally realized something was up when she came into the room. The other four were already there. Will was sitting on the brown leather sofa, Andrea seated on his lap, her thin legs twisted around his. He was holding her around the waist, one long-fingered hand spilling down her jeans, down inside the front of her jeans. Will Gallagher and Andrea Browne were the king and queen of fucking, and they liked to make sure that everyone knew it. Sally walked into the room and noted the look of just-made decision on the faces smiling back at her. In Daniel's case it was more of a smirk than a smile, but then his skin was so bad at the moment Sally wondered if he could smile without it hurting. She started to say something along those lines and then thought better of it. She was late, best she shut her mouth. Ewan leaned against the door frame, stepped aside to let her in and then moved back, pushing the door closed. This was an ordinary Saturday afternoon, his father getting on with some paperwork, his mother making cheese scones in the kitchen, and Ewan well knew that noise traveled fastest when his mother's ears were forced to listen hard. Daniel was sitting on the thick-carpeted floor, his back to Sally and to the door, his erupting face now turned up to Andrea and Will.

It was nearly Sally's sixteenth birthday. This week, Thursday. She knew what they must have been talking about, knew the question she had missed, but not its answer. She had meant to be here on time, had intended to be part of the conversation from the beginning, but there had been an argument at home and her sister was being a bloody bitch yet-a-fucking-gain and then her dad had thrown down his paper and yelled at them both and it had taken ages to get here, waiting for a bus in gray spring drizzle, and now, pissed off and damp, she had arrived. Red-faced and late. Too late.

There was an air in the room, she knew it. They all knew it. Ewan's scone-baking mother knew it too and turned down the kitchen radio to its lowest level, but too late for the closed door. Excitement and a little fear churned into the mix in the sitting room, waiting room.

"I'm sorry I'm late."

"Doesn't matter ..."

"My sister is such a fucking pig."

"It doesn't matter."

"No, but I wanted to be here."

"You were meant to be here."

"I know, that's why I'm saying sorry, all right?"

"Sure."

"I did mean to be here for the talk."

"The talk?"

"Yeah, you know ... you said, Will said ... about me ..."

"Ooh," Andrea mocking, high tone, wounded little girl voice, exaggerated version of the London-edges accent Sally always tried to tone down around Andrea, Ewan's mother, all those other women who spoke low and slow and posh. "About me, Will said you were going to talk about me, don't you all want to talk about me? Isn't everyone interested in talking about me? Let's all talk about Sally, can we just talk about Sally for another little bit? Please? Daniel? Will? Ewan? Don't you all want to talk about Sally?"

This was not new. Sally knew how to take this, be here, listen to Andrea. She was not the victim girl, their victim girl. Not usually anyway, not for years now, not since she'd made her choice plain and clear, to be their friend. Though maybe she was today, maybe now with Andrea having a go. Shit bloody day already and not even lunchtime yet. First her sister and then Andrea bloody Browne, fucking typical. Sally knew exactly what their usual victim did to reinforce this behavior, they all understood the pattern. It was her passivity that encouraged them, she knew it, had seen it, so now she did the opposite, Sally bit back, hit out.

"Fuck off, Andy. My sister has been enough of a cunt today, you don't need to add to it." Talking with more mouth than she felt. Saw it was working. Daniel turned his head to face the group, a grin at the corner of his cold-sore mouth. Will nodded approval from the settee, his fingers still further down the front of Andrea's jeans.

Sally continued with her late-arrival explanation, "I'm only saying sorry that I wasn't here sooner. We said we'd talk about my birthday. And somehow," turning then to Ewan behind her, pointing a finger at his hand on the doorknob, "judging by where Ewan's standing, the way he clearly doesn't want his mum to hear what we're saying, I'm guessing you've already decided on my birthday treat without me, OK, Andrea? So you have been talking about me, am I right?"

Andrea scowled, removed Will's prying hand with a sigh and slid off his lap. Ewan left the door and joined Daniel on the floor. Daniel picked the scab on his lip, the drying cold sore he could not leave alone. He always picked at it when he wanted to be the one talking and Will was holding court. The scab stayed weeping and unhealed.

Will smiled, pushed Andrea away to the other end of the settee and patted the cushion beside him. "Yes, we have. Now stop being so rude to the lovely Andy and come and listen to my story."

Sally crossed to sit between them, picked over the boys on the floor and squeezed into the too-small space left for her on the settee, Andrea seething to her left, Will expansive to her right. Her stomach was tight and tense and Sally thought she might throw up.

Would throw up, but she hadn't eaten since last night, yesterday afternoon actually, thinner in the morning if she didn't eat after five, thinner for their usual Saturday morning at Ewan's place if she didn't eat at all. Never as thin as Andrea Browne though, never quite perfect-girl thin, with her narrow hips and long legs and yet those astonishing still-rounded breasts. Sally sighed inside, brought herself back here and now. This was not the time, yet again, to compare her own body unfavorably with Andrea Browne's. Andrea was no doubt more than ready to do that all by herself.

Will put his arm around Sally's shoulder and whispering, so that the others had to strain to hear, he began to explain the plan.

EIGHT

Saz's few days alone with Matilda were easy. The little girl was on good form, laughing and playing and pulling herself forward in a one-legged crawl—catalog daughter designed to make the child-free yearn for their own, and the already-parenting wonder if now wasn't the perfect time to make yet another. Catalog mother kidding herself the sleepless nights were all in the past and there were no more to come. Not even when Matilda reached sweet suffering sixteen. Or nine, if the pseudo-It-Girl behavior of her middle niece was anything to go by.

Saz spent the Saturday afternoon and night at her own parents' house, being spoiled and waited on. With four other grandchildren well beyond the cute baby stage, Saz's parents were delighted to welcome another small one into their home, take her out to the park, laugh with her for half an hour at a time. Delighted to welcome, and not a little relieved when Saz and Matilda left them in peace, and the prized ornaments and sharp corners could be restored to their rightful places. Despite their best efforts, it had always been obvious that Patrick and Hazel were more than content with each other for company. Enjoying the silence in the lounge, the cooking shuffle coming from the kitchen, breathing in the scent of roasting lamb, Saz's father flicked through the Sunday papers to the weekend's hot story of yet another famous actor and his third young wife having a new baby in the actor's early seventies. He shook his head in horror at the thought of a full-time baby in his own life, checked the clock, and wondered if there wasn't time for them to pop out for a quick drink before lunch. Pint of bitter, brandy and lemonade, packet of salt and vinegar to share. He put down the paper and went to get Hazel's coat.

Saz took Matilda on to lunch with Chris and Marc, where the little girl was indulged by her fathers, and Saz was given a pretty good time too. Then, late afternoon, full of food and just-within-the-limit wine, mother and baby drove home across north London, Matilda, as ever, soothed and sleeping with the motion of the car. Saz enjoyed the time to herself, the flat for just her and Matilda. Molly had always worked long hours, quite often shift work, ever since they first met, and Saz recognized a growing sense of loss at never having their flat to herself any more. Not that she'd ever tell Molly. Or Matilda. Even now, like her own parents, she was setting limits on the truths she'd tell her child. By the time the sun was setting, with Matilda skillfully removed from her car seat in one swift and only slightly-grizzling movement and now fast asleep in her own cot, it was almost like the old days, Saz's own time, and just herself to please. Which she did by settling down for a night in front of the TV with takeaway pizza and a bottle of Diet Coke.

She was starting to doze in front of the new season big expense costume drama—pleasingly populated with a variety of heaving bosoms—when the doorbell rang. She ran to answer it before a second ring could wake Matilda. There was a man standing on the step. Her age maybe, oddly familiar but not. He was wearing a very good suit, had smooth rounded nails on the hand he held out to her. She didn't shake hands. Didn't want to talk to him. Couldn't believe it was really him. Standing there, grinning at her.

"What are you doing here?"

"Hello."

Nothing more. He was smiling, lit by the light spill from the hallway behind her. Smiling at her, at her discomfort she thought.

"What the fuck do you want?"

"I was hoping we might have a little chat?"

London accent, like Saz's, something estuary around the edges, but drawn tighter for the city. Harder. Less real. Less true.

"Why?"

Saz waited for the man to speak. He just smiled. Saz tightened her grip on the door lock, wondered again why she and Molly hadn't got around to putting on a chain. Forced into speaking by his silence, the strength of his silence.

"Look, I'm not working at the moment. I don't … work. Anymore. I mean, if that's what you wanted …"

About to explain about Matilda, her reason for giving up, the public reason, not Molly's reason. Reasons. Stopped herself. Too much information. None from him.

"Not many people do work at this time on a Sunday night though, do they?"

He was still smiling, held out his hand, looked like he was offering a hand to shake, in reality holding tight to the door Saz was trying to close.

"It's Will? Will Gallagher?"

Saz thought she might throw up, pushing against the door, pushing him back. "I know who you are."

"Well, good. Because we need to talk."

"I have nothing to say to you."

As he took his hand off the door, ready to come into the hallway, Saz pushed harder still and slammed the door in his face, double-locking it. He was laughing on the other side of the red-painted panels.

"Ah, really—we do need to talk? Something's happened. We need to talk about it."

"Go away."

He called again, through the closed and locked door, "I'll come back later. Tomorrow maybe, the day after?"

"Go away."

Still under her breath, too quiet for him to hear, leaning with her whole body-weight against the double-locked door he wasn't even trying to open. He was walking off, she heard his footsteps, round the side of the house, down the path and into the street, leaving now, singing to himself a song in French. She hated that song. She'd always hated that song.

Saz leaned against the door for a long time. Eventually she realized she was cold and then remembered she was home, remembered she was grown, and therefore, apparently, she was safe. She pulled herself up from the floor, back creased in door panel indents, went round the flat checking every window, every lock. She sat in Matilda's boxroom, the room they were well aware their daughter would outgrow before the end of the year, lit by the amber elephant night-light, and watched her child breathing, sleeping soundly, until her own heart eased its furious pace enough for her to go back to the sofa and the cold pizza. Saz finished her glass of Coke, toyed with congealed cheese and tomato before she dumped the pizza and went to bed. She lay, eyes wide, staring into the darkened bedroom. The occasional lights of cars passing on the street outside were a comfort. Eventually she slept. She didn't dream. Or if she did, she didn't remember. Saz definitely didn't want to remember.

NINE

Ewan's Mum brought in a tray of food and drinks and the boys fell on it, the girls held back. They took the Diet Cokes, shared a scone without even addressing the issue, smeared away some of the butter, ingested the rest with guilty joy. Didn't want the boys to see them eating. Or not eating. Will slow-smiled his thanks and Daniel started to call her Mrs. Stirling and then mumbled Diane and then muttered nothing at all.

Mrs. Stirling left the room and heard their conversation start up again as she closed the door. Muffled giggles, another squeal maybe. A boy's voice, man's voice, Will probably, sounded like he was making an announcement. Pronouncement. Ewan's mother hoped he wasn't saying something nasty about her. Her looks. Her body. Her age. Ewan's mother went to the kitchen to wash up. She would be forty-one next week. And she knew that was way too old to think Will Gallagher was cute. But she did.

They finished their scones. Put down the Coke cans. Ewan pressed his narrow body hard against the door, listened to the sounds of his mother back in the kitchen, nodded safety to the rest. Everyone looked at Sally; Andrea spoke first.

"Well, are you going to do it?"

Sally paused. Wanted to look as if she was thinking it over. Wanted to look as if she had a choice.

Daniel was picking at that scab again, lip beginning to bleed, Ewan rested against the door now, Will and Andrea were holding hands behind her back on the settee, Will close, his breath on her shoulder, Andrea's body spray perfume strong in her nose, itching her eyes.

Sally shrugged, attempted nonchalance, failed. "Yeah, all right. I'll do it. If I have to."

"Ah, but you don't have to, that's the whole point." Daniel corrected, smiling from his place on the floor. "You have to want to do it. That's the point. Do you want to do it, Sally?"

Sally didn't know if she wanted to do what they were asking of her, couldn't know if she wanted to, it wasn't a matter of wanting, it was a question of safety. Agreeing to the demands of the group because it was always safer to be with them than not. Safer to be of them than not. "Yeah, OK then, I want to."

Will let go of Andrea's hand and moved it up Sally's back and around her shoulders, leaned in closer, whispered right into her ear.

"No, that's not quite good enough. Where's the magic word?"

Sally didn't know what he meant, Will's hand warm on her shoulder. "You have to say please. It's part of the plan." He grinned, close enough for Sally to feel his mouth slide into a smile against her cheek. "And Sally, you know I like it when you say please."

She sensed Andrea's anger beside her, nodded anyway, nodded because part of her liked the feeling of Andrea's anger, lots of her liked the feeling of Will Gallagher this close.

"All right then, I do. I want to do it."

She leaned forward, slid herself free of Will's hand and looked at each of the others in turn—Daniel, Ewan, and Andrea. Then she brought her gaze back to Will. Smiled. Slowly. "Please."

And then Sally smiled again. Because she found she could.

TEN

When Matilda woke at six in the morning, a mumbling semi-chatter, half-song coming from her room, Saz was glad of the reason to get up, follow their established routine, do nothing but care for her child. She called Molly as they had arranged, asked about Asmita, how it was to be there with no Ian, how they were getting on, how it felt in the house. She asked so many questions there was no reason for any others in return. She didn't mention her visitor from the night before. Finally Molly had to go; she and Asmita were driving into Glasgow for lunch and shopping before Molly caught her plane home. Asmita had decided it was time to buy a new duvet. Molly knew it was the right move—Ian had always been too hot at night, her mother too cold. She also thought the shopping was heartbreaking; she wanted her mother to behave as if nothing had changed, when everything was different. Molly thought it was too soon for her mother to change her bedding. It would always be too soon.

Saz hung up reluctantly and when the phone rang an hour later she ran to it. Then stood in front of the gray handset, not wanting to answer. If he had her address, then maybe Will Gallagher had her phone number too.

Probably he had her phone number too. She didn't pick up and then the answerphone kicked in, but no one left a message. When Saz dialed the ring-back number she found the caller had withheld their number. It could have been anyone. But she didn't think so.

The sun was shining beyond the tight-closed windows and the warm day, just on the twist into proper autumn, would normally have had her out on the heath with Matilda in half an hour. Her pre-baby routine of daily running had, since Matilda, turned into long fast walks for the two of them. Today, mother and baby stayed inside, doors and windows still locked.

Matilda didn't mind. There were good games at home and a more than usually attentive mother who was interested in anything that might take her mind off things, anything at all to still her chattering brain. Every nursery rhyme Saz knew and then they started all over again. Practicing their favorites for when Molly came home. Saz practicing Matilda's favorites. And not even nearly bored this time, she gave ten renditions of "The Lady and the Crocodile" perfectly happily. When Matilda went down for her sleep after lunch, Saz went to bed too. Took her daughter into the big bed with her; she didn't want to be alone. No one else called other than Molly when she was at the airport and ready to board the plane home. No one came to the door; the only post was an electricity bill and the menu for a modern Indian restaurant, same old dishes at newly exorbitant flock-free prices. The flat was quiet. Saz kept quiet. Tried not to listen to the past reasserting itself.

When Molly was safely home, had kissed and lightly stroked her sleeping daughter, they sat together and talked through the past few days. Molly's journey, Asmita's crying, at first stilted, scared to start, and then again and again. Taking the ashes up to Loch F'yne, leaving Ian there, father ash and rose petals floating off on the water's surface. She told Saz how it had felt in the old house. Home but not home. And yet, how Ian seemed to be in every room anyway. The jams and green chilli pickle he loved in the pantry, his favorite koftas and the lamb casserole still in the freezer. The shock that her mother, that healthy appetite in the sweet round woman, had no interest in food. It was good she'd lost weight, Asmita had wanted to lose weight for years, Molly knew it was good for her body too. But now she'd done it and her husband wasn't there to see. Ian could look after himself, five years as a merchant seaman had taught him that much, he had cooked as often as Asmita had throughout Molly's childhood, made dishes his wife loved, taken care of her. She just wasn't interested now. And when Molly made one of Asmita's favorites as a treat for both of them, spent four hours on the sauce, slow bubbling, neither had been able to eat, just sat at the old wooden table crying. And drinking. Whisky, wine, water. Molly told Saz it had been good, crying together, getting pissed together. Molly, tears streaming down her face, said she felt better than she had in ages.

And all that evening Saz nearly, almost, not quite, told Molly about the visitor. She didn't know what to say, where to begin. How to go back there, to a place where she had been so unhappy, tell Molly a brand-new story about the past Saz chose not to remember herself. Saz didn't want to tell that story. She was scared that speaking it aloud might bring another knock on the door, Will Gallagher returning to her home. So she sat beside her partner and listened and kissed her lover's fingers and laughed at the stories of Ian and Asmita's friends, helpful and loving and consistently clumsy, no good words to make death better.

They went to bed early that night, at ease in each other's arms, with each other's bodies. The days away turned to kisses in bed at home turned to kisses on bodies at home turned to slow fuck and fresh delight and just Saz and Molly, the two of them, as they had been so good at for years now. Easy fuck, soft into welcome sleep.

Then the phone rang.

"Shit!"

"Leave it."

"We can't leave it, Saz."

"Yes, we can. Ignore it. Pay attention to me." Saz pulled Molly back to her side.

"But it's late."

"Let them call back in the morning."

"It might be important."

"This is important."

"It might be my ma. We can't leave it."

The phone was ringing on. Saz realized she must have forgotten to switch on the answer machine, and now Matilda had heard it and started wailing, and Molly was up and out of bed and halfway down the hall. "For God's sake, Saz, what's your problem? Get the bloody phone. I'll get her."

Then Saz was sitting up and the phone was in her hand, fingers over the mouthpiece. "OK. Fine. OK."

She felt sick, scared of talking to him again, scared of Molly asking questions. She held the receiver in her hand, almost to her ear, not quite there, not quite ready. She could hear the expectant waiting on the other end, someone waiting for her voice, her answer. Not ready at all, acting ready. Hoped sounding ready might do it for her, where looking shocked and horrified yesterday certainly had not.

"Yes? What is it?"

There was a delay, then a small voice, a woman's voice, not his voice. Saz thought of Ian, of Asmita ringing Molly, of the too-early-morning call and the sickening bad news. Nothing good ever came of doorbells and phone bells at the wrong time of day.

ELEVEN

"Saz?"

"Yeah? What? Who is it?" Still nervous, not trusting the familiar female voice on the other end of the line.

"Saz, it's me, Claire. What kind of a greeting is that?"

Relief, anger, annoyance, adrenaline flooded through her body and out her mouth. "Claire? What the fuck are you calling at this time of night for? Where are you?"

A pause, then, "Oh yes. It's night there, isn't it?"

Saz looked at the green glowing clock on the desk. "Midnight, after midnight."

"Right. And you always answer your phone that nicely?"

"Yes. No. Are you OK? Why are you calling so late?"

"Sorry. Didn't think. I'm at work."

"And I'm not. What do you want?"

"I want you to do a job for me. Just a one-off, someone I need to check on in London, for a client."

Saz sighed. Claire Holland, old friend, big party queen, very successful solicitor, had left for New York several years ago, moving from one department of her sprawling firm to another, finally giving up business law and settling in the only slightly less lucrative but way more interesting area of family law. Divorce her specialty. Nasty, messy, huge financial dispute divorces her special specialty.

"Claire, I'm not working. I'm being Mummy."

"Still?"

Claire didn't get it. She didn't want to get it either; she wanted Saz to work for her.

"Yes, still. Permanently. For a while, for the foreseeable future. She's only nine months old."

"Yeah, but the money would come in handy, wouldn't it?"

"Yes, no ... Molly's earning enough for three of us for now. We're lucky, and then again, we're not quite as high maintenance as you either."

"True. Last time we met I thought you could do with a manicure."

"Yeah, and I thought you could do with two less martinis."

"That'll be after the four each we'd already had?"

"Claire, please, it's late. You know I don't want to work anymore, I gave up. I'll get another job when Matilda's a bit older, when I work out what the hell I want to do."

"Don't you mean what the hell you can do?"

"Yes, that too. Right now I'm very happy living a nice quiet peaceful life."

Safe life. Saz wanted to say safe life. But she didn't want to tempt the gods who had so generously given her Claire on the phone instead of someone she really didn't want to speak to.

"Ah, but this is a nice quiet peaceful job."

"No such thing."

"No really, just listen. It's this new client of mine. His marriage is over, she left him, he's been the carer for years, she's the one with the big career and all the money. She's refusing alimony, says she can't afford it, and we don't believe her. I need someone over there to have a look, check her out."

"Yeah, and even if I wanted to do this job, she'd just let me into her house and the office and her bank account, would she?"

"Doubt it. But she's saying she can't afford to run her car or pay her bills, let alone the expenses my client's been left with for their home here. She says she can't even manage to eat out once a week. And my client happens to know this ex-wife spends every Tuesday and Thursday afternoon at a very expensive girlie lunch with her college mates, then on to one of those pretending-to-be-New-York spas—though God knows why; no one really cares about the state of their body in London anyway."

"I do."

"Not extending to weekly pedicures, you don't. And even if you did, you wouldn't follow it up, as this woman does, with a nice speedy shag-fest, getting herself seen to by one of the harder working boys in town."

"Does that mean hard working or working boy?"

"The latter. Of course. Though he probably works hard at it too."

Saz was pulled in despite herself. "God, different world, isn't it? Is that why they broke up?"

"Nope. My client's gay, the wife's known all along and it suited them both, she had the money, he looked after her and escorted her and saved her from having to admit to being yet another single woman in New York. Except now he's fallen in love and finally decided it's time to come out, and she's being difficult about money because she's pissed off with him."

"Right. So when does she find time to earn all this money if she's off being pampered all the time?"

"I think, sweetie, when you're as wealthy as she is, it's more about investments and handling portfolios than anything as crude as actually having a job."

"So they're rich?"

"Filthy."

"Then what's his problem? Can't your client just go to work himself?"

"Parity, darling. We can't say a dumped wife deserves alimony for taking care of the husband for thirty odd years if we don't offer the same for the men too, can we? All I need is proof that she's still doing any one of those things, though all three would be best, and then my client puts in his final claim. On Friday afternoon. When the wife flies over for their next meeting. Hence the urgency. If we present her—and her lawyer—with proof that she's still spending loads on the silly stuff, then she can't keep saying no to my bloke."

Saz sighed again, heard the wails of her increasingly irritated daughter, Molly losing patience down the hall in Matilda's room.

"Maybe she can't, Claire, but I can. I'm not doing it. I'm going back to sleep. If Matilda will let me. If you'll let me. Goodnight?"

A pause then, Claire thinking of the best way to try one more time, and leaving it just too late.

"I'm hanging up now, Claire. 'Bye."

Saz put down the phone. Heart rate returned to normal. Screaming baby, not happy Molly. Home returned to normal.

Matilda was still wailing on Molly's lap. Saz took her from Molly.

"Sorry."

Molly offered a questioning look. Saz shook her head.

"Claire. Offered me a job. I said no."

"Good. Cup of tea?"

Tea drunk and it was now one-thirty in the morning, Matilda wasn't the least bit tired, Saz and Molly were both grumpy. After half an hour trying to pacify Matilda, they took her to bed with them where she promptly fell asleep, hot arms and legs spread as far as her nine-month-old body would allow, pushing Saz and Molly to the far edges of the mattress. A truck drove past outside their ground-floor flat, shaking the house from the foundations up.

"These houses weren't built to have that kind of traffic going by."

"No."

"One day the whole bloody place is going to fall in on top of us."

"Yeah."

"And Matilda's room is way too small for her now. It's so full of stuff."

"Yes. I know."

Saz didn't care. She couldn't stop thinking about her visitor from the day before, trying constantly not to, glad of the distraction Claire's phone call had provided. Glad and already interested and trying not to think that Claire's offer sounded like fun. An easy day's work, a simple day's work. Matilda sleeping soundly now, Molly wide awake and not enjoying it.

"Saz, please don't look like that."

"Like what? What look? How can you see anyway?"

"Because I know how you think. You've got your I-can-solve-the-world's-problems look."

"Didn't know I had one."

"Well, you do. And anyway, you know what I mean."

Silence then. Molly worrying on her edge of the bed. High wind blowing about the trees that made up part of their back fence, hundred-year-old house creaking out the stories of middle-of-the-night floorboards.

Saz forced to break into the dark. "What?"

"It's different now."

"Yes. I know."

"You've always put your work before me …"

"That's not fair."

"No, you have. And in a way it was OK, before. My work was really important to me too."

Saz's whisper turned hard. "I haven't done anything for well over a year. Year and a half. I've been here for you ever since I came out of hospital, I've been supportive with all the stuff about your dad, I've taken care of you."

"I'm grateful. But you just said it …"

"What?"

"Since you came out of hospital. You promised you wouldn't do anything again that might harm you. We have a child now, it's different."

"I know it's different, that's why I feel it so much more. I look at all the shit things in the world and I can't help being terrified that any one of them might happen to Matilda. And I still want to make things better."

Molly sniffed, "Right, and Claire's work is about making things better? So she's left that job where she makes money out of rich people's misery and is now saving the world?"

"No, but she is trying to make little bits of justice, in her own way."

Molly was silent again. Turned over. Then carefully back to Saz, Matilda undisturbed between them.

"I start work full time this week. You know I can end up working late sometimes, there's always something they need one of us to stay late for. If you take on this job for Claire, what do you intend to do about Matilda? Because there's no way you're taking her out with you on a wild goose chase."

"Of course not."

"I find it hard enough leaving her, Saz. I don't think I can stand the idea of neither of us being with her."

"Moll, it's irrelevant. I told Claire I wouldn't do it. You're going on about this for nothing. I already said no."

"But you'd like to."

Another silence, acknowledged truth slipping out into the dark.

"Maybe. You wanted to go back to your work."

"My work doesn't always seem to involve people trying to hurt me. At least not since I last worked nights in A&E. I just want to keep my family safe as well ... what's left of it." Molly added slowly, "I don't care if that sounds selfish. I want to put us first, all three of us, always."

"Yes. I know."

They stopped then. Quiet and dark. Listening to Matilda's easy breathing between them, the wind outside ripping unready leaves from the trees. In agreement and not at all.

TWELVE

One of the things that astonished Saz about becoming a mother was how incredibly long everything now took. She'd heard other parents moan before, how every journey was a mission, and she'd thought they had to be wrong. How hard could it be? You had a bag and your baby and that was it. Saz wasn't sure why she'd imagined she might suddenly become perfectly organized simply by virtue of getting an egg to agree to the attentions of a passing sperm—she'd certainly never been that together before—but she had figured it couldn't possibly be so hard. And then Matilda came and Saz understood. Not the reasons why, she still didn't know why it was that every time she tried to get out of the house with her daughter something seemed to go wrong or get in her way, but she knew for sure that she'd become one of those parents. The one with everything sitting on the back doorstep and ready to load into the pushchair. Everything except the baby. She hadn't yet left Matilda in a shop, but she no longer thought it was too far-fetched a possibility.

This morning though, was different. This morning Molly was starting back at work all week, and in the space it took her partner to wash, dress, drink two cups of coffee and eat three thickly buttered slices of burnt-to-black toast, Saz had fed, washed, and dressed Matilda, and showered and dressed herself by the time Molly had her own things ready.

And all the while the morning routine was undercut with the combined tensions of Molly's first full-time day and their unresolved conversation of the night before, with an extra determination for Saz that she get out the door before any unwanted visitors came knocking again. Though she did admit to a growing interest as to why he'd come. Interest and fear—two of her more usual emotions. Molly didn't need to repeat her view; Saz knew well enough exactly what her partner thought about her becoming involved with any of Claire's work.

"I'll see you tonight?"

"Yep."

"No, it's just … well, you know."

"Molly, I'll see you when you get home. We'll both be here, safe and sound."

Molly sighed, not wanting to get into it again, not wanting to leave it unfinished. She chose to be nice, make nice. "Thank you."

"For what?"

"Understanding how I feel."

Saz's tone was crisp, she wanted Molly to go. "It's fine. Done. Good luck."

"What for?"

"The beginning of a whole week's work? Being a big girl?"

"Oh right, that."

Then Molly was gone and Saz stared around her, at the messy kitchen and her ready and waiting daughter, slowly relaxed her shoulders, let out her held breath, realized she had made her choice without even noticing it. She reached for the phone.

The phone rang in New York; Saz left a message on Claire's machine. Five minutes later a barely awake Claire called back. Another ten minutes and the phone rang in Carrie's flat, the one she'd been subletting from Saz for years now. Saz left a message. Within half an hour an emailed attachment of several pages had arrived. Saz printed out photos and addresses. The phone rang again and now Carrie was talking, croaky sleep voice edged with wakening interest. Saz explained her story and just over an hour later Carrie was standing in Saz's kitchen, a half-eaten Mars bar in her hand and a wicked grin on her face.

"Just one thing, Carrie, I don't want Molly to know you're here today."

Carrie finished the last mouthful of the caramel topping and threw the mangled nougat half into the bin. "Why not?"

"I just don't, OK?" Seeing the resentment on her ex's face, she added, "It's nothing to do with you, it's just … you know …"

Saz could feel the smirk even though her back was turned and she was pulling on her jacket.

"Of course I won't let Molly know I was here instead of you. You know how much I love it when you lie to her."

"It's not like that."

"Sure it's not, but you do have a story just in case? To explain why I looked after your daughter all day?"

Saz grabbed her car keys and bag. "I thought maybe I just wouldn't bother."

"I see. Sin of omission rather than commission?"

"No idea, sweetie, we lapsed Protestants don't care so much about the definitions." Saz was playing along, much preferring to bat the idea back than acknowledge the complicity. "You're sure you know what to do with Matilda?"

"Feed her, play with her, put her to sleep, change her if necessary, feed her some more, watch telly. Maybe in that order. How hard can it be?"

Saz looked at her daughter's face, the slight yawn and simultaneous frown indicating a looming tetchiness. "Good question. You can let me know later. And don't answer the phone. Molly will call my mobile if she thinks we're out."

"What if she comes home unexpectedly?"

"She won't."

"She might."

"No, she won't. Doctor Steel has precious little lives to save. Very important job."

"Well I have daytime telly to watch, so piss off."

"Good luck."

"You too."

Saz heard the first of Matilda's wails as she reached the footpath. Part of her felt guilty and wanted to run back. Part of her knew her daughter had had a disturbed night and that Matilda tired was simply Matilda tired, no matter who was holding her. And part of her was happy to be walking out of the flat. She got into the car and drove away.

THIRTEEN

Maybe we could become friends again. Not that we were that close before, not that you ever gave me a chance before, with your funny looks and arty knowing and your clever—so clever—mouths. But hey, let's let bygones ... be. All of you with your lovely lives and charming lovers and whole new worlds, partners and babies and engagements and weddings and families and moving on, always moving on. You have something of mine. You have my past. Each one of you has denied it and hidden it and pretended for so long that it didn't happen, you almost made me think so too. Certainly everyone else believed you. But I know better now. And I want it back.

FOURTEEN

Checking out cleaners was always easy. Saz had been a cleaner, it was the easiest of her post-school jobs when she was wasting time between finally deciding not to go to university and what else it was she wasn't going to do. Wasn't going to be a lawyer, wasn't going to be a doctor, wasn't even going to be a teacher, all those dashed parental hopes despite the holy grail of an attained grammar school education—wasn't going to be a nurse, hairdresser, bank manager, soldier, plumber, chef either. Wasn't going to do any of the things her parents or teachers or sister had suggested she do. Not that she wanted to do nothing. Saz did want to earn her own money, had no desire to slump in front of the telly all day, and even less desire to become a career waitress like most of her sister's university mates seemed to be doing. She just didn't want to do anything that actually sounded like work. And didn't know what an alternative career might be, or how to find it. Cleaning houses for rich people filled the gap perfectly. Even when the rich people weren't all that rich, just two jobs and too many kids and not enough time and employing a cleaner was a damn sight easier than fighting about who did what every weekend. Though some of them were loaded. It gave her cash in hand and got her out of the house. And, eventually, it gave her an inkling of what might become her proper job—the person who finds out the things you don't want them to know. And sometimes, don't even know you want to hide.

By the time Saz had half a dozen regular jobs, she realized that not only was she incredibly skilled at cleaning a four-bedroom house in three hours—while charging for five—she also knew all she could ever want to about her various employers. The unused

51

sheets she washed from the guest room when her boss had asked her to change the sheets specifically for the old friend who was coming to stay for the weekend—an old friend who was coming to stay while his wife was away. The uneaten healthy foods thrown out after a week in the fridge and the rubbish bin loaded down with takeaway containers, pushed to the very bottom of the bin by the woman who could kid herself she was on a diet, could kid her boyfriend she was on a diet, but certainly couldn't kid Saz. The failed pregnancy test sitting in the bathroom rubbish bin, open desk diary indicating heartbreak or heavy-sighed relief. Yet another depressed coffee cup left beside a rumpled, uneasy bed, the morning's whisky dash still scenting the dregs. Saz found she knew way too much without even trying. And then she found she liked knowing so much and tried harder. Eventually she turned uncovering secrets into her proper job. But she never forgot how much the cleaner knew. Which is where she started with Claire's client's ex-wife.

Laurelle Cottillo was out at work; Saz had checked with the office secretary, Ms. Cottillo was in a meeting all morning. Newly reclaimed gay sexuality or not, the soon-to-be-ex husband had still behaved like a traditional bloke during their relationship, and had left his wife to take care of all domestic arrangements in their London home. He offered the suggestion that the cleaner came from an agency, that she was Spanish—or Portuguese maybe—and that was about it.

Saz waited outside the house for an hour and then, when the cleaner had set the alarm and was leaving, jumped out of the car and introduced herself as the manager of a rival agency. She told the Brazilian woman that she'd heard good things about her and suggested they stop for a chat. Maya played up a pretense of interest—as long as Saz was stupid enough to think offering a free coffee and cake down the road was a sensible way to get new workers, Maya wasn't going to disabuse her. The cleaner was on her way to another job; she'd have needed to stop for lunch anyway. If she agreed to chat, this woman would pay for the food and drink, and Maya would get out of the rain for a while.

Saz told Maya about her own start in cleaning. Told her true stories of stupid clients and greedy clients and just plain dirty clients. And in return Maya, at first circumspect and then happy to talk, told her own truths. The bloke who'd taken her on and hoped she'd offer more in his bedroom than just clean sheets. And she might have as well, if he'd have been better looking. The old woman she cleaned for weekly whose daughter employed her as much as a companion as a cleaner—easier for the daughter not to have to clean her mother's home, or talk to her mother except on the phone. And then Ms. Cottillo. Still having Maya come in three times a week so there were clean sheets every second day and the bins emptied faster than any mess could be made. Booking Maya as often as before, but paying her just once a week through the agency and the other two days cash in hand. Good for Maya and good for Ms. Cottillo, who needed to keep some things private from her ex. Saz paid for the sandwiches and coffee, bought a chunk of extra thick coffee cake to take home for Molly and, having taken Maya's details—name and number for her own invented agency—they parted at the door, neither woman looking back.

Saz went back to the car, did her best not to eat the cake—though smeared her mouth with a couple of fingerfuls of icing instead—and waited while the rain continued its incessant rooftop drumming. Half an hour later the cake was gone and Laurelle Cottillo came home, just as her husband had told Claire to expect—mornings at work, lunch with her girlfriends, and then the afternoon at home. An hour later a young man bounded up the rain-slippery steps. After ninety minutes he came back out, carefully closing the gate behind him. Saz left her car and followed him along the quiet residential street, through the park and into the High Street. As he headed into another café she started to wonder what the hell she was doing, and worse, what she was going to say to him. She liked how it felt, not knowing what was coming next.

He bought an espresso, water, low-fat muffin. She had a cup of tea. He settled down on the empty sofa in the window. She sat on the armchair opposite, dripping umbrella propped against the chair leg. He started to read the *Guardian* he'd pulled from his bag. She read the writing on the walls. Meaningless aphorisms about the joys of coffee. He looked up, she looked up. She smiled. He didn't. She smiled again anyway. Saz watched the big-city mask settle over his features, the don't-talk-to-me face she usually wore in public, the one Carrie didn't even know how to pretend, the one Saz would hate Matilda to get used to.

And then she smiled a third time, launched in. "Hi."

She saw his shoulders flinch, watched his eyes lift from his paper to hers, offer a reciprocated greeting and then back again to the page, quick as possible so as not to encourage the intrusive stranger.

But Saz had enjoyed her morning and wasn't going to be put off that easily. She started again, London accent and antipodean tourist attitude.

"I was just wondering ..."

"Yes?" Still weary, still annoyed, but maybe slightly interested now.

Saz pointed to his paper. "The girl section?"

"The what?"

"G2. Girl section? Could I ... just while I have my tea? If you're not reading it right now ..."

He wasn't. Nor could he pretend he was. He was on the letters page of the main paper. Obviously.

"Yeah. Sure." He handed it over. Relieved. A chunk of newspaper. This part was easy. She just wanted to read. Reading he could do, quietly, alone. She didn't want to talk. Yes she did.

"Have you known Laurelle Cottillo long?"

"What?"

"Laurelle? Didn't I see you leaving her house?"

"When?"

"Just now, wasn't it you? I thought we came down the street together?" He stared at her, Saz pressed on, "She's my neighbor, I'm over the road. I'm sure I've seen you going to their house before, Laurelle and Bart's ... haven't I?"

Their house. She made it safe for him. Offered information. He wasn't speaking out of turn.

"Yeah. Laurelle and Bart."

"Right, and you're their ... gardener?"

54

Saz glanced over to the window. It was still pouring down outside, just as it had been all morning. He looked out the window and back at Saz. And then, very obviously, he looked her body up and down, smiled, lowered his voice.

"No. I'm not the gardener."

"Oh?"

"I'm Mrs. Cottillo's personal trainer." He stressed the Mrs., still smiling. "It's my job to make her sweat. She's American, you know. They prefer to sweat when they exercise, not like English girls, all yoga and no effort."

"Right. So what do you do instead?"

"I work my clients."

"Right."

"Really hard. But then, I'm an osteopath too. I know how to take care of the body."

He was flirting. She'd expected him to be closed or defensive. Angry maybe—she had asked for his paper after all, what he probably wanted was an easy post-shag coffee, she'd disturbed his routine. She'd anticipated pissed off at least—instead he was quite obviously flirting with her. Maybe business was slow, maybe she looked like she needed a workout. Saz wondered if perhaps she should get back to running, if the walks with Matilda weren't making enough impact on her flesh.

By the time she'd finished her cup of tea, Saz had Damien's business card, a rundown of his costs—from a one-off personal assessment to his yearly rate for long-term bookings, and an offer for a free trial workout. She promised she'd get back to him. The prices seemed pretty high for a trainer, even for one who—according to Damien—brought all his own gear and would be happy to meet you seven days a week, anywhere at all, in the greater London area. His costs were maybe even high for sex, she wasn't sure, but his manner was outstanding. And if she'd been looking—and wealthy, and straight—Saz might well have taken him up on the free trial offer. As it was, she went back to the car with a spring in her step—flirting was flirting, wherever it came from. She called Claire to say that she'd fax over the price list as soon as she got home. No matter which of his services Damien was giving Laurelle Cottillo, even at the lowest rate for long-term clients, he certainly wasn't cheap. Apparently very available, but not cheap. Saz drove slowly home through the school-run afternoon traffic feeling satisfied with herself. Blatantly obvious flirting from a very attractive young man who was maybe as much as a decade her junior had done the new mother no harm at all. And neither had a day's dishonest work. She'd fax his price list to Claire, email the story she'd had from Maya, and expect a not insubstantial sum in her bank account in three days' time. And it was only just four o'clock.

When she let herself into the flat she was surprised to hear Carrie talking, not in the baby-talk high pitch she usually employed to keep Matilda amused, but the lower, more serious tone she generally reserved for sexual conquests. Saz's immediate thought was that Carrie had asked the new lover to visit, and she sincerely hoped that she was not about to walk in on her ex in anything but a compromise-free position. She'd had more than enough of Carrie flaunting her desirability at any given moment. She called out hello to give them a chance to rearrange themselves and just as she had her hand on the door handle she heard Matilda's giggle—and another, far more disturbing thought came to her—what if Molly had come home early after all? And, if that were the case, which particular lie had Carrie been entertaining her partner with, and would she be able to pick up on the clues in time?

Saz pushed open the door, took in Carrie on the sofa holding a cup of coffee, another half-finished cup on the coffee table in front of her and a man sitting beside her. Both fully dressed. Both clearly pleased to see her, both smiling up at the horrified woman in the doorway. Will Gallagher was holding Matilda, bouncing her on his lap. Matilda was holding tight to his thumbs, clapping her hands as he clapped his.

He spoke over her daughter's curls, softly spoken word kisses ruffling the baby's hair. "Finally! I thought I'd have to go before I got a chance to see you."

And Carrie added an accusatory, "How could you have known Ross Gallagher all this time and never told me?"

"His real name's Will."

"Now you tell me, I've told you all about my famous friends. Well, all the ones I've shagged anyway!"

She and Will laughed together, giggling, knowing. Clearly their coffee cup bonding had been very successful.

Will ruffled Matilda's curls, mouth smiling, eyes sharp, daring Saz to contradict him, "Yes, but we go so far back I expect you've forgotten you ever knew me so well. Am I right, Sally?"

FIFTEEN

Sally was sobbing. Wanted to be out of here, out of this. Anywhere but this. That thing she'd seen on TV, the documentary about those fucked-up anorexic girls, most of them her age, that thing one of them said, about how she cut herself. The voiceover lady called it self-harm, the expert talked all about it, made sense of it. She wondered if that might do it for her, like the woman in the prison film on TV, make it better. Make it go away. Make them go away. And she'd been here so many times before, felt like this—this useless, this hopeless, this misunderstood. This fucking stupid. God, she felt so fucking stupid. Her sister said she was being stupid. Only her sister meant it differently. Nothing was that bad. Except that Sally thought it was. This was that bad, this was as bad as it got. Looking round her bedroom, wondering if now was the time to get on with it. Get on with leaving.

Anyway, she hadn't really told her sister everything. Just that it was getting worse at school. There were some other kids, you know how it is. This group, a couple of boys, some girls. She let her sister picture the rest, let her practiced schoolground imagination build up what she wasn't saying. Anyone could imagine, everyone's been to school, goes to school. Everyone knows what it feels like. It feels like shit. Every fucking day. Day after day. Five days out of every seven. But Sally wasn't telling her sister the whole truth. Couldn't tell her the whole truth. Not ever. Could barely stand to admit the truth to herself. She'd told her sister there was this bunch of kids, giving people a hard time, even hassling one of the new teachers too, new teachers always so easy to give a hard time, always so easy to scare. This bunch of kids that everyone knew about and no one did anything. No one

58

ever did anything; that was what she found so amazing. No change.

They'd talked about it the night before and her sister had been sympathetic for a bit, but only a while. Said all the right things, the things big sisters were supposed to say. But Sally knew her sister was bored too, wanted to get on with her own stuff, homework, tea, TV, diary, telephone. Every night the same routine. The sister had calls to make, friends to talk to, a boyfriend she really needed to be talking to. Some shit going on there, something the sister didn't yet understand and wondered if he was going to tell her the truth or talk around the problem again like he had yesterday. Whatever the problem was—and she still wasn't sure she wanted to know, not if the problem was her. She really liked this one. Properly liked him. Not just a boyfriend so she could say she had one, but a proper boyfriend. Anyway, truth was she couldn't exactly be bothered, not that much, not with her little sister's shit. Fuck, everyone has their problems, deal with it.

The big sister assumed the little sister must have been getting a hard time too. Said it happened to everyone. Because it did. Everyone knew it did. Everyone's life had some bastard bully in it at some point; all you could do was ride it out, hang on and wait for it to pass, for them to pass, the cloud of them, crowd of them passing on and over to another unwilling victim. Big sister checked the time, something to watch on TV, phone call to make, bored now. Left the bedroom and pointed out that if the little sister really was going to top herself, or do something fucking stupid like cut herself, then best not to do it in her bedroom. All those clothes on the floor, the ones she hadn't bothered to put away for days, they might get dirty. And some of them weren't Sally's actually, some of them had been borrowed from the big sister's room and not returned. That top's mine for a start. There are worse things in the world, Sally. War, famine, flood, drought. Way worse. And at least you're not fat.

Sally watched the big sister go and was relieved she hadn't told her everything, lay back and waited and listened to the nervous twisting of her stomach and found she was pleased to have told her almost nothing. Sally was glad she hadn't told her sister exactly how badly she wanted to get away from these other kids at the

59

school, how much she needed to get as far away as possible from this thing that was happening to her. She kicked her foot through a pile of clothes on the bed, watched as they fell to the floor in a slow-motion spray.

Glad she hadn't told her how really fucking hard it was to be one of the bad guys.

SIXTEEN

Saz felt a wave of shock run through her, a deep lurch at the pit of her stomach, cold chill tumbling down her spine. She held out her arms, waited for voice to follow the action. Eventually the words came, "Give me my baby."

"Saz?"

Carrie was confused, didn't understand her friend, looked from Saz to the famous man sitting beside her, the recognition running between them, his ease with Matilda, Saz's repetition.

"Fucking well give me my baby."

"Saz, what's going on?"

"Go home, Carrie."

"What? What's wrong?"

"Just go home. I'll call you later. And you," directing her voice but not her eyes at the bemused man, "you wait there. I won't be long."

She snatched Matilda from his hands and practically ran from the room, her daughter screaming at the speed and fury with which she'd been wrenched from the warm arms of the nice bouncing man.

Over the strident screams of her daughter she heard them saying goodbye, Carrie telling the visitor how nice it had been to meet him, how sorry she was to leave so quickly. Carrie came down the hallway to Matilda's room, Saz standing holding Matilda tight to her, the wailing baby refusing to be pacified.

"Saz?"

"Carrie, go home."

Carrie's confusion came out in her sharp tone, "I didn't know I'd done anything wrong. He said he was an old friend of yours, he said you went to school together."

"Yeah."

"Well, he can't have been lying. He knows loads of things about you, told me about your mum and dad. He knows Cassie."

"Yes, he does. He did."

"So he is an old friend?"

"No. He is not an old friend."

"Oh. Oh well. Shit." Deflation of tone, "I'm sorry. I thought it would be OK. He said you were expecting him, and I figured maybe you'd just forgotten, he did know all of you. I'm really sorry ..."

"It doesn't matter. I just don't want to see him."

"Is it a bad time? Shall I tell him to go?"

"Look, I'll sort it. I just don't want him in my house. Our house."

Carrie, thinking she understood what this was all about, said, "Oh. Right ... so is he ..."

Saz laughed then, Carrie's typical assumption bringing her back to a safer place, a usual place, "No, he is not an ex I forgot to tell you about, definitely not that. Go home. I'll call you later. And thanks for taking care of Matilda."

"How did the job go?"

"Fine, all done."

"Good. Well, we had a nice day. Matilda loves Oprah. And those makeover programs. We watched three in a row. And I taught her to say 'I love you Auntie Carrie.' She'll do it for you if you ask really nicely."

"She's too young for that, Carrie."

Carrie looked at her, frowning, "Yes, I'm joking, Saz."

"Oh. Right. Sorry."

"Sense of humor deficit?"

"Something like that."

"OK then, right ... 'bye."

"Yeah. Sure."

Carrie left the room and Saz stood with her daughter in her arms, slowly rocking the fury out of her child, balling up her own anger into a more manageable state. She checked the Bambi clock on the wall, the same one she and Cassie had had in their shared bedroom when they were really small, second hand permanently pointing to the tip of Bambi's curled tail, hour hand making its way past five o'clock. Molly wouldn't be home for another couple of hours. She had time to deal with this. Now was the time to deal with this. He was here, in her lounge, waiting. Saz put her daughter down in her cot, covered her with the blanket and placed Wool Bunny within arm's reach. Saz studied the toys around her; she realized she knew the provenance of each one. Toys put away and kept in hope, others hurriedly grabbed on the way to visit the newborn, given with love by fathers and family and friends. And the only one Matilda was even slightly interested in turned out to be the misshapen rabbit made by Cassie's youngest daughter. And Will Gallagher was still in her lounge. Bambi said five-fifteen. It was time to face him.

He was sitting on the sofa, reading a book. He looked up and smiled at her. "I thought I might have to wait, brought a book for the car. I didn't expect to be let in so easily. Or to have such a nice chat with the delightful Carrie. You really shouldn't have let that one get away."

Saz knew what he was saying. That Carrie had outed her. Unwittingly no doubt, without even considering what she was doing, without thinking it mattered at all. Saz wouldn't normally have thought so either, though she preferred to out herself in general, but it unnerved her, what he seemed to know about her life already, what else he might know.

"I didn't let Carrie get away, she dumped me."

"Ouch. Lost the babe. That must have hurt."

"It did for a time, though I don't imagine she'd thank you for that description."

"Oh, I don't know, I think your little friend knows exactly the effect her clothes and style have on men. And women. Teenage boys and blind men, I imagine. Can't think why she'd dress like that if she didn't."

"Whatever. I don't expect you're here to talk about my ex-relationship with Carrie. Or your reading habits."

"Ah yes, but I'm a very intelligent man these days. The thinking woman's crumpet. At least that's what the *Mail on Sunday* said last weekend."

"Never buy it. What's the book?"

"Gogol."

"Really?" Saz couldn't hide her surprise. "Which? There are more than one, right?"

"I believe so. *Dead Souls*." He held up the cover for her to see. "There's talk of an adaptation."

"Yeah, well, I can't imagine even you would pick up something like that for light reading. Though you always did have incredibly pretentious taste."

"Anything to take me away from that suburban hole …"

"And will you be playing the dead soul or the other guy?"

"Whichever pays the most, darling."

"Yes, I've seen some of your work."

"Thank you."

Saz cut his smile, "I'm not sure that's a compliment."

Gallagher took her denial with a complacent nod. She continued, "Why Ross?"

"The other Will Gallagher was a variety performer, so I needed another name. Out-named by a bloody juggler. Ross was my nan's maiden name. You know, Nana Tilly?"

Saz looked at the man in front of her. Thrown by the memories. "I don't really care, I long ago stopped connecting the man on the screen with the boy I knew at fifteen."

"And sixteen. Seventeen too, weren't you?"

"Not quite, I turned seventeen a few months after I left school. You were one of the reasons I left so early."

"So your lack of further education is my fault?"

Saz spat back, "What the hell do you know about my education?"

"My nan talking to your mum, they always liked a good gossip."

"That was years ago."

"I didn't forget."

"Well, I've done my best to forget you were ever in my past. We're all different people now. And you're on TV so much I'd never be able to sit in and watch a night of boring dross if I was worried about seeing you all the time, would I? I choose not to connect the bloke in fancy dress with the one I knew then."

"So you're easily impressed by televisual fame?"

"Not a lot." Saz sat down in the chair opposite. She looked at him properly then. Took in the nice suit—nice, not flash, comfortable, not fancy, the careful highlights, shaped brows, clean-shaven skin. Nothing too smooth—good looking but not pretty. "You come across really well on the box. All those strong but understanding speeches, loving husbands, complex, honest citizens. Bastard with a heart of gold. You do them really well."

"They write the lines for me, you know."

There was silence then, Saz still not ready to hear why he was there. Not wanting to hear why he was there.

He started to speak and she quickly interrupted him. "Your accent—when did it get so ..."

"Common?"

"I don't know. Sort of. I mean, some of those kids we were at school with were pretty posh, but all our parents wanted us to do better, they all had that grammar school push going on."

"I did do better."

"Yeah, but your better sounds like their worse."

"I know. My nan used to say so too, hated it. Especially when she was wanting to show me off to her mates. Still, makes for much stronger parts, everyone likes their good guy to have a bit of rough these days."

"They certainly get their rough with you, don't they?"

Gallagher wasn't going to let her get to him, acknowledge her baiting; he continued on his own train of thought, "You ever visit her, Sally? My nan? When you go to see your mum and dad?"

"No one calls me Sally anymore and my parents don't live round there now."

"Yeah, that's right. They moved out. But Cass does, doesn't she?"

"What do you know about Cassie's life?"

"Nothing. I'm just thinking about family. You know, extended family, family and friends, those people who aren't really family, but treat you like it all your life anyway? So you never go and see

65

my nan when you visit those nieces and nephews of yours? Grew up next door to her, all those years, in and out of her place whenever you wanted, and now you can't even pop in?"

"Oh, fuck off." Saz wasn't interested in engaging in conversation with him, least of all about an old woman he rightly suggested she had once cared for and had chosen not to see for years. "Your nan doesn't need the likes of me popping in when her grandson is one of the more famous men in Britain."

"Yeah, but she thought the world of you."

"Yes. She did." Saz nodded, at him and her own thoughts, "And she was wrong wasn't she? She thought the sun shone out of all our arses and she was wrong. We didn't deserve her approval, not one of us, and you were the worst of the lot."

Gallagher looked at her. Waited. Eventually he nodded. "Fair enough. And that's why I'm here. She's been trying to get in touch with me. She wants to tell the whole world just how bad we really were."

"Who? Your nan?"

"My nan's got Alzheimer's. If you'd ever bothered to visit her you'd know she's been fucking bonkers for the past five years. Knows who I am maybe one visit in every ten, if I'm lucky."

Saz's hand went to her mouth, involuntary exhibition of her sorrow for the old woman she had indeed been fond of.

Gallagher went on. "No, it's not my nan, I wish it was."

"Well, who …"

Saz stopped. Stared at him. Mouth dry, adrenaline bitter in the back of her throat.

Gallagher nodded. "Janine Marsden called. She's left messages on my answerphone—fuck knows how she got my number. She sent letters to an address I thought was totally private. Says she wants to talk. Though from the way she put it, I'd say she wants to shout."

SEVENTEEN

Saz felt sick, hot, cold. Very sick. Pictured Janine Marsden coming into the school playground every morning, back into their arena, the one where they were in charge and the likes of Janine Marsden simply had to put up with it. Janine Marsden coming into the school grounds that morning, that last morning, and how horrified she'd been that instead of just running into the building with everyone else, running and hiding and keeping out of the way, Janine was coming over towards them. Walking right up to them. Saz who was Sally hating what was coming, terrified of what was coming, and unable to do anything to stop it.

"What does she want?"
  "She wants to talk to us."
  "You and me?"
  "No. All of us. The five of us. You, me, Andrea, Daniel, and Ewan." He listed their names and Saz's stomach lurched again, the familiar litany of who she had been, what they had been together, rushing back to her.
  "She wants to talk to Ewan too?"
  "That's what she said."
  "But I don't understand, how does she ..."
  Gallagher was still talking. "Janine Marsden says she wants to have a chat. With all of us. I don't know how to get hold of the others, how would I? I've been trying to work out what the fuck to do for the past fortnight. And then, God, I don't even know who told me now, maybe my nan before she completely lost it, but last week I remembered someone telling me ages ago that you did this kind of work."

"Did. Don't do anymore."

"That's not what Carrie said."

"What?"

"She told me you were working today."

"Well, she shouldn't have. It was just a private favor for a friend." And Saz reminded herself to fax the price list to Claire. Reminded herself about her real world, matters of insignificant divorces and court cases over too much money. Molly at work. Molly coming home from work. Carrie's big mouth.

"OK. But this is a private thing too, don't you think? Janine Marsden? She's threatening to talk about me."

"Oh."

"And I don't know anyone else I can trust with this."

"You're scared about your career?"

"Primarily. But there's also the small matter of my getting married at the end of the year."

"That wasn't in the *Radio Times.*"

"We're keeping a lid on it for now."

"Anyone I know?"

"Not personally, but you've probably seen her on TV."

"Actress?"

"Investigative journalist."

Saz nodded, understanding. "And you don't want her investigating you?"

"Not if I can help it. But it's not just about me, most of the stuff she's really successful at has to do with crusading cases from way back in the past. I wouldn't want my past shit to taint her either."

"How very chivalrous you've become, Will."

"I'm in love. It changes things."

"So call the police. Tell them you're being blackmailed, get them to sort out Janine."

Will glared at her. "Are you being deliberately naive? How the hell do you think the tabloids get half their stories anyway? The cops are the last people I'd go to with this. Anyway," Gallagher paused, and Saz wondered how rehearsed his speech was, "it's not only me, is it? I mean, I know I'm the famous one, that's why she got in touch with me first, but Janine Marsden can't talk about me without talking about you too. And I don't imagine you've told your partner, what's her name—Molly? Is that what Carrie said? I don't suppose you've told her all your stories. No one ever does." He waited again for his words to sink in and then added, "Or have you?"

Saz looked at him, understood Will Gallagher as well as she had done years ago. He was waiting with all the confidence in the world, knowing her answer. Will and Saz both knew that neither of them would ever be prepared to share these secrets with anyone else. She wanted to kick him out, close the door, walk away and pretend none of this was happening. Instead she answered his question.

"No. I haven't. And I won't."

Saz knew she had no choice. She also knew time was getting on and there was plenty she needed to do before Molly arrived home from work. She agreed to meet Will the next day and found herself shaking with relief when she slammed the door behind him. Working on automatic, she got through the next ninety minutes. Matilda could be counted on to amuse herself for about twenty minutes before the primary colors and squeaky noises of her baby gym became infuriatingly dull, so Saz called Claire first. As the phone rang she knew she could at least be grateful that the urgency in her tone would make sense to Claire's New York secretary and she wouldn't have to put up with a London temp's version of efficiency. She followed the fast phone call with a detailed email, faxed through Damien's price list and her own invoice, impatiently cursed technology while the digital images went through, and then took Matilda into the kitchen. There she alternated between renditions of "Incey Wincey Spider" and preparing the pasta sauce that any world-working woman might reasonably expect her child-caring wife to come up with—especially when she had nothing else to do on an early autumn afternoon.

By the time Molly came home, Saz had not only created appropriate scents in the kitchen mess, but she had also managed a whole thirty minutes playtime with their daughter—almost long enough for her Will Gallagher–induced terrors to recede slightly in her pleasure at Matilda's daily growing semi-vocabulary. Though she still flinched when Molly rang the doorbell. Her hands full of tube-journey novel and work bag and the big bunch of flowers she'd bought from the florist by the station, Molly couldn't make it to the bottom of her bag for her own keys. Fortunately Molly was so full of her own day that she barely even noticed the look of uncertainty when Saz opened the door. They put Matilda to bed, ate, shared a bottle of wine, and left the dishes for the morning. In bed, Molly tried to explain to Saz how torn she felt between work and their child, and Saz lied about the day she'd spent with Matilda, lied about what she'd done with her afternoon, and lied about what she planned to do the next day. They kissed and held each other and quickly fell asleep, exhausted, fingers crossing in the dark.

EIGHTEEN

The next day Saz and Matilda had lunch with their unwelcome guest. Over his decaf, skimmed milk lattè, Will filled in some of his history.

"When we were at school you said wanted to be a TV presenter?"

Will nodded. "Yeah, for a while I thought it would be a better use of my talents."

"And?"

"I was shit at it."

Saz shook her head, Gallagher didn't understand, "What?"

"Nothing. I'm just surprised to hear you say you were shit at it. I'm surprised to hear you say you were shit at anything—that's hardly how the Will Gallagher I knew would talk about himself."

"We all grow up, Sally. Saz."

"Yeah, but I'm also surprised that you weren't good at it. All our teachers, parents, you had them eating out of your hand. Surely that's the perfect manner for a presenter?"

"Thank you."

"Only you would think that was a compliment. You always knew exactly what to do to get people where you wanted them. You had it down perfectly. Not to mention adding in sexual charm for the girls when you fancied it."

Gallagher grinned, "I had no idea you had such a good impression of me. I'd have tried harder if I'd have known I had a chance with you."

Saz just looked at him, refusing to join in his old-mates routine. "We were talking about your work?"

"Yeah, well, turns out fooling the people in your bland little suburb isn't quite the same as fooling them on screen. I discovered very early on that apparently what the public want from proper presenters is truth, not lies."

"Whereas what they want from actors is …"

"Simulacrum of sincerity, sweetie. Nobody's perfect, but you know what? We can all try."

Gallagher smiled his famous rueful grin, shrugged his wide shoulders, and ran a hand across his trademark tousled hair. Dark blue eyes and slightly crooked smile, just-healthily-tanned skin beginning to crinkle at the laugh-line corners. His gaze totally on her, Saz knew exactly what his employers and his very many fans saw in him. Even she could feel herself warming to the classic representation of a lovable rogue sitting opposite her. She blinked and thought back to the Will she'd known, trying to recapture the exact mix of attraction and fear. It wasn't hard—clearly he'd just taken those qualities and smoothed them out to suit his successful career. The butter-wouldn't-melt-in-your-mouth nice guy crossed with an *Eastenders* thug when he didn't get what he wanted.

"So you chose Ross because it was your nan's maiden name?"

"I thought it was a nice gesture; she liked it."

"You really did have a soft spot there, didn't you?"

"Everyone's got one, Sally. I found yours quick enough."

Saz's voice was hard again, "What do you mean?"

Gallagher nodded at Matilda, dozing in her buggy beside them. "All this happy family shit. Pretty damn suburban really, you at home with the kid, the wife out at work. Hardly the stuff of radical lesbianism, is it?"

"It isn't a political choice who I fuck, never has been. That's not what this is about at all. Molly and I are just working out how to be with a kid. We don't know yet, this is a start."

"Yeah, but you're not really happy, are you? Much as you might like to settle down and play the good little wife?"

"You know nothing about me, Will."

"I'm not talking about your sexuality, give me some credit. You're hardly the first dyke I've ever met. Not to mention that I had a pretty good idea back then as well."

"Bollocks."

"Why else did you never come on to me? I've always been aware of how people see me, I know you think I'm an arrogant bastard …"

"Yes."

"But I do know what was written about me in the girls' loos."

Saz was flung back to fifteen and rainy days, the primitive cartography of toilet walls way more interesting than geography ever could be. "How?"

"Andrea told me."

"Andrea probably wrote it."

"She'd never do that."

"Not unless you told her to."

Gallagher stopped then, leaned back and sighed, smiling, "My point is, I guessed you were a lezz ages ago. And not just because you didn't want me, though lesbianism's never stopped half the actresses I know fucking blokes for show, but the fact is I'm a very good judge of character. And yes, maybe just a little bit arrogant as well."

"Nicely put. So if you're not making assumptions about my politics, what are you talking about?"

"You weren't at home when I came calling yesterday. Much as you might say you want to, you aren't completely playing the good little wife."

"We don't do the role-playing thing."

"Who does? But that's not what I was talking about."

"I told you, I was doing a favor for a friend. That's all."

Gallagher smiled and Saz wanted to hit him. "So Carrie said." She wanted to hit Carrie too. Will continued, "And now I need you to go to work for me as well. And for yourself." He paused, waited for an answer he knew was not coming, and continued, "Because while I accept that right now my concerns might be more pressing than yours, I know you don't want to expose your past truths any more than I do. So let's just get this crap with Janine sorted and out of the way. Then I'll fuck off and leave you in peace."

Saz opened her mouth to tell him he was wrong, that he had no concept of her relationship, of her life, that she had none of his worries. And then she stopped, feeling the ripple of fear in her stomach, the excitement she only felt from potential danger. The whispered risk of hidden secrets. Even if those secrets were her own.

Will might need to keep his past from the press and his bride-to-be, but Saz had always maintained there was no breaking point that her relationship couldn't take. Now, with new-old pictures in her head, she questioned that assumption. She didn't want to tell Molly any of the things she'd been forced to remember in the past couple of days. Saz had never talked about Will and Andrea and the others, not to anyone, not to Carrie even, certainly not to Molly. She didn't talk about that morning or the events leading up to it. Especially not the events leading up to it. She didn't talk about it and she didn't think about it if she could help it. Had trained herself not to think about it through years of denial and repression. And now, here was Janine Marsden—via Will Gallagher—bringing it all back again. Of course she couldn't tell Molly.

A middle-aged woman approached their table, asked Ross Gallagher for his autograph, took a good long look at Saz and Matilda while he was signing her coffee-stained paper napkin, and then giggled her way back to her friends on the other side of the café. Matilda began to stir, soon to wake for her bottle, and Saz made the leap.

"All right then. Who do we contact first?"

NINETEEN

It took Saz a little over an hour, masquerading as three different girls from their grammar school, to register on several variations of Friends Reunited. She was about to give up and get on with making lunch for Matilda when it occurred to her that she hadn't yet tried her prime source. She called her mother. The phone call was not good timing.

"Can't I call you back, Sarah? I'm just getting the beans up for your dad's lunch."

"It won't take long."

"Patrick had a lovely lot of beans this year; we froze most of them. Would you like me to keep some for you? Very good for Matilda, lots of iron."

"Yeah, Mum, thanks. Look …"

"Though you probably buy all yours organic, don't you?"

"Ah, yes. I mean we do … if we can …"

"Total waste of money. I was telling Cassie just the other day, it's all a con, you know. Of course, Molly's doing well in her job, but with only one of you working, you should take more care. They know what you lot like, you know."

"Us lot?"

"Young mothers. It's all guilt-tripping, advertising's to blame, no one even knew about organic food when you two were little, didn't do either of you any harm. I remember you used to love those tins of processed peas."

"Mum! OK. I'll take some beans. Next time we're over."

"All right then, I'll put some aside. Now you must let me get on, your dad's starving."

"No, wait, I called for a reason."

"Oh?"

"You remember Daniel Carver? Who I went to school with?"

"Judy Carver's boy?"

"That's it. I need to get hold of him. Someone mentioned a reunion thingie."

"I wouldn't have thought you'd be interested in anything like that, you were so glad to leave that school, you couldn't get away fast enough. And we were so proud when you got in ..."

"Yes, I know, Mum." Saz covered. "And I don't know that I am interested really. It's just this thing, I heard about ... anyway ... do you know what he's doing now?"

"You know I do."

"Mum, how would I know?"

"I told you all about it; why don't you girls ever listen to me? I bumped into Judy Carver when he was just starting to retrain."

"As what?"

"A teacher, Sarah, I told you. Full of it she was, how well he was doing, what a good move it would be. Well, you know how she used to go on and on about him when he moved to America. Quite the big filmmaker she said he was, doesn't sound like that panned out though. Still, must be much nicer having him home near her."

"He lives in England?"

"Judy said he'd moved back out that way, over where we used to live. She's still there too, I think. Houses are so much cheaper if you don't insist in living in the center of town ..."

"Yes, Mum, we know. Do you know where he's working?"

"I think Amy had him last year for something or other ..."

"Amy? Daniel's teaching at Amy's school?"

"Not anymore. And it's not a school, it's a college, sixth form college, Amy's very touchy about that. I told you last time you were over, Cassie said she hates it when we call it a school. She's very particular about it. Not that I can tell the difference. Although I don't know if she still wears a uniform ..."

"Mum, what else did Judy Carver say?"

"Oh, you know, the usual 'my boy' fuss. She's always indulged him, that one. Apparently he was the drama teacher. At the college. Who'd have thought a boy like that would become a drama teacher? Thought you'd need to be a bit more sparky for something like drama. I remember him as a quiet boy, clever yes, but quiet. Not like Ross Gallagher—did you see him last week?"

"What?" Saz was horrified.

"He was on breakfast telly, talking about something he's done. Still good looking, isn't he? Still full of himself too if you ask me ..."

"Yes, Mum, please, Daniel?"

"Oh yes, well he was at Amy's college and then he moved on. But she might know where to. They seem to know so much these young ones, don't they? Not that you and your lot were any different of course. Or you could ask Judy? I'm sure I've got her number somewhere."

"No, I don't think so, I'll try Amy first. Mrs. Carver still scares me. She was always so ..."

"Judgmental?"

"Yeah. And arrogant. Looked down on us."

"She still does. I take it with a pinch of salt. I'll ask her if you like?"

"No, really, it's fine." The last thing Saz wanted was to get Judy Carver's version of Daniel's new life. She couldn't imagine Daniel was any more truthful with his mother now than he had been when they were younger, nor did she want him to know she was trying to find him. Surprise had always been a better way to deal with Daniel Carver than reasoned argument. "Thanks, Mum. I've got to get Matilda's lunch now too. I'll speak to you later, yeah?"

"All right then, lots of love to your ladies."

Saz's subsequent conversation with her niece Amy was far faster.

"Why?"

"I think I used to go to school with him."

"You did."

"How do you know?"

"You went to that school near your old house, right? Where you and Mum grew up? They made it into flats?"

"Yeah."

"Well, he said he did too. And he must be about your age. He

77

told one of the girls I know. Like it would impress her, that he comes from round here and then went off to America. He thinks he's so cool because he made some fuck-off film in New York or something and then when he can't get work anymore he comes back here. And becomes a film studies teacher."

"Mum said it was drama?"

"Whatever. Maybe both. I don't know, I don't do that stuff. Anyway, why do you care?"

"I just thought it might be good to get in touch with him again."

"Oh, Saz, don't, he's a wanker. Everyone hates him. He was going out with one of the girls in his class, that's why he left school."

"Really?"

"That's what I heard. When the other teachers found out he had to move."

"Where to?"

"How would I know?"

"Well, maybe I could I talk to her? The girl he was going out with? Could you arrange for me to meet her?"

"Could do. I'll find out. But I don't think you'll like her much."

Two days later, Saz left Matilda with Carrie again. Carrie was exhausted from three nights playing with her new fling and very happy to spend an afternoon in, and Saz made her way over to her London-edge home ground. In their telephone conversation, Saz had told Will she thought it was very lucky Daniel Carver should have moved home to teach, and even more so that he was having an affair with one of her niece's friends.

Gallagher's theory was that it had nothing to do with luck. "No, both things are typical Daniel. He might have had that one success, but he's always been the kind of guy who's far more comfortable in a small pond than a big one. And there's no pond smaller than the one you grew up in."

"So how does that fit with him having a relationship with a student?"

"He had his big success young. And nothing since then. He's

probably one of those people who'll spend the whole of their thirties wishing they were nineteen again. Then again, if this girl is young and eager ... who could blame him?"

"Fuck off, Will. Blokes always think it's fine for another man to go out with a woman years younger than himself. I bet you wouldn't be so keen on the idea if Daniel were seeing a boy student instead of a girl."

Will shrugged, "Might be right. Doesn't negate my point though; he was always way happier when he could kid himself he was in charge. I doubt that's changed."

Saz couldn't disagree with him, but nor was she keen to get involved in a dissection of Daniel Carver's failings. It was all too clear to her that anything either of them could say about Daniel's aberrant youthful behavior twisted straight back to their own. They agreed Saz would find out what she could about Daniel, and Will suggested the two of them should try to meet up with him together.

"Safety in numbers. You know, he's as likely to want to see you as you were when I turned up on your doorstep."

"You make it sound like I'm OK about seeing you now."

"No, I don't. But we don't have a choice. If we want to stop Janine Marsden telling all—and I take it you do?" Saz flinched, her stomach twisting as unbidden pictures flashed into her mind. She couldn't answer, but Will was pressing her. "You do want to stop her talking, right, Sally?"

She let out a quiet "You know I do."

"Good. Then we're all going to have to get to know each other again. Daniel just doesn't know it yet."

Saz was about to hang up when another thought occurred to her. "Have you heard from her—from Janine—since last time?"

"She called last night. I told her I was on to it, but she needed to be patient. I said that getting the lot of us to meet up after all this time wasn't going to happen overnight."

"And?"

"She repeated I've got until the end of the month to get us together and then to see her, or she'll go to every newspaper and radio station and TV news reporter in the country. Thereby fucking up my wedding, my career, and everyone else's happy little lives as well."

"Is that what she said?"

"In as many words. The bit about everyone else's life is mine."

"I thought it might be."

"Listen, Sally, if you think I'm going to let her fuck it all up for me and not the rest of you, you've got another think coming."

Saz laughed, "Believe me, Will, I'd never think that of you."

"Good. So we've got until the end of the month."

She looked at her watch. "That's two weeks away."

"Twelve days."

"Shit."

"Indeed."

They were quiet then, until Saz ended their conversation with a final question. "And she did say all of us? All five?"

"Yep, she was very clear. You, me, Andrea, Daniel and Ewan."

"Oh."

"She asked about you too."

"She did?"

"Specifically. I told her you were my first port of call. She sounded pleased."

Getting to the sixth form college was easy, Saz knew the route backwards, had walked past the building often enough throughout her childhood. Twenty years ago it had been the grotty boys' school up the road from the grotty girls' school that she would have far preferred to go to, much preferring a supposedly bad school with most of her mates, to following her sister to the grammar school full of posh kids and rich kids and other kids just too damn clever for Saz's liking. But she did get in, and Hazel and Patrick were determined she go and take advantage of the chances neither of them had had. Since then there'd been a shifting of local borough priorities, a slew of financial cutbacks, the girls' school was knocked down to make way for an expanded shopping mall, the boys' school rebranded as a sixth form college, the grammar school turned into luxury apartments.

Saz's parents had long since moved away, further out to where buses were less frequent and hills more common. Cassie and her family had moved back to the area eight years earlier when property prices were on the edge of a leap and moving out of the central city meant they could exchange their three-bedroom flat for a whole house, with garden. The classic London compromise—central urban versus suburban sprawl. Cassie had promised Saz she'd understand the need to move out of town when she had more kids, wanted space and good local state schools. Saz had promised Cassie she'd understand the desire to stay in the city when she was one half of a lesbian couple with a Scottish-Asian partner, a mixed-race baby-father, and a brown baby.

Getting to the college was easy; walking up the street full of students was not. While she was often told she looked young for her age, Saz realized as she walked that the people who said so were mostly around her own age—neither they nor she had looked at her reflection recently from the perspective of the average seventeen-year-old girl. A girl to whom all women over twenty-five were in that nebulous range between mother and crone, where around thirty might as well have been around forty, maybe fifty, not quite sixty. The middle ages as seen from the middle teens.

Saz realized when she pulled up near the school and parked round the corner that the nerves she was feeling were to do with hoping she might pass. She hadn't really thought what she intended to pass as—an older sister perhaps, a potential teacher come for an interview, fairly young and not-too-distant, easy to talk to, to confide in. But one look at the young people milling outside on the street told her she'd got it wrong. In the street outside the school buildings, where a storm of sixteen-, seventeen-, and eighteen-year-olds were gathered for their own lunch, Saz was as painfully obvious as if she were a ten-year-old trying to fit in reverse. She walked slowly up to the first group she came across, all too aware that in trying to look like them she looked even more different. She'd have done better to wear a suit and pretend to be a journalist, a sensible skirt and nice shoes and come as one of their mothers or a history teacher. They might ignore her just as easily, but they weren't likely to both ignore and threaten in the same moment. As they were now doing. As she walked towards them. As the tallest of the perfectly highlighted girls turned to face her. And started to laugh.

TWENTY

They laughed at us, that first day going to big school. All those other kids and some of them so grownup, they looked like adults, like teachers. And we weren't like most of them, not skiing-holiday material, her or me. But we had got in, had a right to be there, that's what my dad said to her mum. And we knew each other sort of, from primary school, and our houses weren't too far apart, so we walked there together. Then time passed and they all laughed too loudly and then she joined in, was like them, became one of them. They were different too, but different on their own terms, their own choice. The choice to stand out, in torn black jumpers, reading books no one else read, movies no one else watched, music everyone else hated. They made their own place and then she was with them and I wasn't welcome anymore. So they weren't laughing at us, they were laughing at me, and she was laughing with them. I tried to behave as if I didn't care. But I did. And she knew I did. And she laughed with them anyway.

Of course I know why she did it, I'm not stupid. She saved herself. They were never going to stop and she understood that sooner than I did—she was always way cleverer than me. So she went over to them, joined in with them, perhaps she really did like those boring fucking foreign films they used to watch. And she was probably right to go to them, maybe I'd have done the same. Or maybe not.

There are some new choices to make now. I wonder how they'll decide what's right this time?

TWENTY-ONE

Saz heard the laughter first, then looked up at the group in front of her. It all flooded back as she stealed herself to keep walking, recalling as she did the ghastly teenage years of working out who to be and how, finding herself in a group of misfits who eventually turned weird into cool-select by force of desire as much as anything else. Force of Will's desire, of Daniel's, and she just hanging in there as long as she could, scared to be part of them, scared to be apart from them. Scared and hiding it—as they all had—with black-and-blue clothes and a don't-care-anyway carapace.

Standing beside them, adult eye to teenage eye-liner and allowing herself to look at the various groupings of young people with adult awareness instead of many years' worth of her own fear of massed youth, Saz allowed herself to breathe out, she realized this lot weren't too bad. There were the obvious idiots, the ones she'd have hated to have been at school with herself. The kind of kids she'd learned about within her first term at junior school, the ones she quickly learned to get on with as soon as possible so they had no reason to pick on her for the rest of their shared days. Nine to four is a long day in which to suffer, and Saz had been better than many at appearing to fit in when all she felt inside was how little she matched the others. Now of course, with adult knowledge, she knew that no one, not even those who seemed totally at ease, had ever really belonged. Every grownup she knew admitted to feeling apart, not only during their childhood, but in much of their adult lives as well. The difference was that while not fitting in, being different, standing out, was ghastly for most children, for many of the adults she knew, it was now how they earned their living. For the likes of Carrie, individuality was prized and praised—but not until the school gates had long closed behind them. Saz walked past the first group, eyes down, color up in her cheeks, and twisted away from the image of herself at the same age. There were a couple of noisy boys and louder girls, increasing the volume of their conversation as Saz passed, certainly for her benefit.

"No! You didn't?"

"You fucked her?"

"You must have been so off your face."

"We had some speed. So?"

"Yeah, well she must have been really pissed to shag you!" Chorus of laughter, of sly looks, Saz moving on. And even as she thought it, she looked round for some wood to touch and save her from Matilda becoming a moody grumpy sixteen. Or worse, a sly-mouthed seventeen with an eager chorus of her own.

She rounded a group of lads, none of them prepared to step out of her way, Saz was forced off the curb to get by, and then presented herself to a couple of girls standing off to one side, together alone. It only took three texts from the ever so helpful—for five quid—Hannan to Eleanor to Ysmahan before Saz was directed to Becky. Who, everyone knew apparently, would be in the pizza place for the second half of lunchtime. Saz followed their directions and went to wait, turning down the house offer of a teacher-special lunch deal as she did so. Clearly the new old-look jeans, pink gingham All-Stars, and dark purple T-shirt she was wearing marked her out as yet another teacher. Saz was disappointed. Despite the kids' reaction, she'd thought she looked better than that.

Twenty minutes later, Becky Allicott came in with a small group of girls, most of them looking a little younger than Amy. But not Becky—at that distance she looked a very grownup seventeen. She left her friends hanging by the door, sat down in front of Saz, and shouted back over the counter for a skimmed milk latte. Up close Becky still looked grownup, but it seemed more of a look and less of a truth. Saz was forcefully reminded of Daniel Carver at that age, pushing hard against the boundaries of child and adult and not knowing where to stop. She found herself wishing Will was with her. Will was the kind of man—even without the fame of his Ross-incarnation—who would have this girl wound round his little finger with one curling gesture. But his fame was exactly the reason he wasn't there. And she was.

"I'm Becky. Amy said you wanted to speak to me? You're the aunty, right?"

Saz flinched inwardly at the aging term, one her nieces and nephew were forbidden to use, but smiled anyway. "I'm Saz. Hi."

Becky nodded. Grinned back at her friends, gestured them closer in. Maybe she wanted witnesses for her audience with Saz. She was evidently delighted to be sitting there, though for no clear reason Saz could see.

"So how can I help you ... Saz?" Slight pause, too big a grin.

"I just wanted to ask you a few questions."

"Something to do with school?"

"No."

"But it is about Mr. Carver? Daniel?"

"Yes."

"So what are you, the ex-wife?"

"I didn't know he had one."

"Neither do I." Then a little laugh, making sure her audience had heard her, "But I don't think you'd be wife material, even if he did." A louder laugh now, spreading to the other girls.

Saz held her tongue. And the hand that wanted to grab Becky's and make her sit still, face front, stop turning to her gurning mates. "No, I'm an old friend of Daniel's; we went to school together."

"So why don't you speak to him?"

"I don't know how to get hold of him."

"I do."

Saz was still calm, quiet, "Yes, I know."

"You could ask his family. They still live round here."

"Daniel's mother didn't like me when I was at school with him, I don't imagine she'd approve of me any more now."

The girl sat back in her seat, studying Saz. "Were you a bad influence?"

Saz shook her head, remembering the long lectures Judy Carver had given her own mother about her son's perfection and how little his friends lived up to him. "She thought so."

"But you want to get hold of him now?"

"Yes."

"Why?"

"It's a long story."

Becky was clearly enjoying the power of her special knowledge. If this was the kind of easily led baby Will had imagined Daniel being with now, Saz hated to think of the girls who were too tough for Daniel to handle. She took a slow breath and hoped that the pause would give her some of the status Becky seemed intent on keeping to herself.

"Let's just say I want to get in touch with him, but I'd really like it to be a surprise. I thought if I find out where he goes for a drink or something like that, I could just turn up. From what I hear, you probably know more about him than I do these days. He was your teacher, after all."

"Yeah, but ..."

"What?"

Becky shook her head, "Nothing. You probably just think we're all a lot ... younger than we are."

Saz looked at Becky's long highlighted hair, straightened to an icy sheen, the rings on her fingers, heavy-handed makeup, perfectly shaped and shaded nails. "Only in years."

It was evidently the right response. Becky softened considerably. A mirror-perfected grin curled her beautifully defined lipline into a pout of shaded maroon. Saz imagined this girl had probably never gone over the lines in her coloring books. "So what do you want to know?"

Becky was obviously eager to tell Daniel's story—the young girl-friend keen to show how very much she knew about her bloke. Not that she actually admitted to having had an affair with him before he left the college; even in her desire to show off to both Saz and the listening friends; she wasn't stupid enough to admit to that kind of trouble. She did, though, manage to pass on the basic details of a few of his great American adventures—no doubt somewhat embroidered for the benefit of her young woman's impressionability. She offered a brief description of his teaching style—all right, pretty good really, if you care about that shit. Becky didn't. And best of all, the pub Daniel liked to drink in after work. Every day except Fridays, when he went to a first-run movie up in town. Saz was surprised to find herself smiling to note that even after his own career disappointments, Daniel couldn't keep himself away from other people's work. Even if it was only to slag them off as Becky suggested.

After she had paid for their coffees, and the ones Becky's friends had ordered as well, Saz stood up to go, asking as she did why Daniel Carver had been so interesting to Becky? Weren't any of the guys at college worth seeing?

"Some are. Some are all right. But they're just too young for me. You should ask Amy—one of the slightly less shite ones wanted to go out with her ..." One of the standing girls poked another in the ribs. She was studiously ignored. "But you know, she wasn't really interested." The pouting smile again, nearly a laugh. "In fact, we were wondering ..."

"What?"

"Well ... you know ... maybe ...?"

Becky bit the perfect upper lip, picked at the edge of one of her dark pink nails, raised her eyebrows with her inflection. More stifled giggles from the chorus line behind.

"No, I don't. Why don't you tell me?"

Saz had no idea what they were trying to insinuate and the teenager before her suddenly morphed into a talk-show host, all fake-attention and concern.

"Well, we wondered if Amy was ... like ... you."

Chorus line eyes wide, Becky's lipline held tight against a mouthful of sneer.

Saz looked up at the backing four, held their gaze until they looked away, turned her attention back to Becky. "Oh, I see. You thought Amy might be gay because I am?"

"Well, not just because of that."

"No. Also because she wasn't interested in the guys you think she should fancy?"

"Well, yeah."

"Boys from this school?"

"This college. Yes."

"The ones I saw outside? On the street by the gate?"

"Yeah, some of them."

"Spotty, greasy hair, concave chests, bum-fluff faces? Not really grownup yet? No proper sexual experience, no skills to speak of, nothing that would make a young woman moan in pleasure and surprise?" The chorus line leaned even closer. "Those boys?" Saz underlined the word boys.

"Not all of them look that young."

"No, not all of them do. But they all are that young, aren't they? I mean, you're not interested in them, are you?"

"Yeah, but that's different, I've got ..."

Saz continued, ignoring the gap where Becky couldn't risk naming Daniel as her lover. "Yes, I think we both know exactly who and what you've got. I hate to tell you this, Becky, but it takes a bit more than not being interested in seventeen-year-old boys to make you a dyke."

Chorus line giggles and Becky furious with her back up, "I do know that actually."

"In fact, it generally takes wanting to fuck other women."

Gasp from the chorus, defiance from the lead.

"Yes. I know."

Saz couldn't help herself, reached out and patted Becky's arm, "You do?" She left with a wink. "You know? I imagine you do, Rebecca." And a very sweet smile.

TWENTY-TWO

That night, Saz and Molly made dinner together and bathed Matilda and talked about their respective days. Molly told how she'd saved a three-year-old's life, counseled a grieving father, and completed a small forest worth of paperwork. Saz told lies. The two women then sat down, again together, exhausted in front of the TV. There was nothing on. Literally. The set wasn't switched on but they sat facing it anyway; neither of them had the energy to get up and turn it on, despite the fact that Molly had already expressed interest in *Newsnight*'s trailed piece on the MMR vaccine, and Saz was hoping that the look at tomorrow's papers would show a front cover featuring Ross Gallagher's whirlwind marriage to a Brazilian supermodel, previous plans in tatters; Gorgeous Gallagher's sudden conversion to radical Buddhism; Rugged Ross's untimely death in a freak costume drama horse riding accident—anything that would get him out of her life, rid her of her present fears. She knew it was stupid—even without Will around, Janine Marsden would have to be dealt with. Saz had always been highly skilled at charging into other people's problems; she was starting to see just how good she'd also been at running away from her own.

Saz was sitting beside Molly, had spent the entire evening by her side, and felt anything but together with her partner. And she was about to take herself further still.

"Babe, do you mind if I go out tomorrow night?"

"What?" Molly stirred herself from her thoughts of baby guilt versus patient guilt to pay attention to her partner. Partner guilt.

"Do you mind if I go out tomorrow night?"

"No. Why? Where?"

"Nowhere yet. Don't know. I'm just feeling a bit hemmed in, being here all day with Matilda."

"But you said you went for a big walk today?"

Saz, not wanting to lie any more than was absolutely necessary, had indeed told Molly that Matilda had had a big walk that afternoon. Which she had, with Carrie—when she'd realized three hours away from her latest delight was two hours too long and had walked Matilda to a café where she and the new love-hope had flirted over baby, tea, and cake.

"No, I mean proper going out. I'm sorry, I know it sounds awful, and it's not that I'm not happy at home with her, not at all ..."

"But you're feeling stir-crazy?"

"Yes. No. I mean ..." Saz sighed, allowing her self-imposed angst to be interpreted as a reluctance to admit being just that little bit constricted by the new routine with their daughter.

"Sweetie, of course you should go out and do something nice. I'm sorry, I'm coming home totally knackered and I can't be any more interesting for you than a grumpy nine-month-old."

"No, it's not that." Saz knew if Molly was too nice she'd want to tell the truth even more. "I just fancy a night out. I'm sorry. We could do something together? I could ask Carrie to babysit?"

Saz knew the offer was a risk. Will might not be free to meet up with Daniel the next evening. Daniel might not be in the pub on his usual night out, Becky might not know Daniel as well as she thought she did. All of it risky, but while Saz could be sure of nothing to do with the people she had once known so intimately, she figured she did know Molly well enough to take a chance.

"Or it might be nice for us to go out together? I know it's your first week back, but ..."

Saz was right. Molly's head was shaking before she even finished her sentence. "I just don't think I can face it. I won't be able to get up in the morning, and it's not as if Matilda lets us lie in anymore. You go out, see if Carrie wants to do something, or one of the boys. I'll stay home with her. It'll be nice for me anyway; we don't get enough time together alone now. I'm jealous that you get to take her for a walk and I don't."

"I'm sorry."

She meant it both for her partner missing their daughter and for her lie. "No, it's cool. I'll see if I can finish work a bit early. Then I can do her tea and the bath stuff, you can get off out."

"You sure?"

"Yep. It'll do you good." Molly stood up, turned on the TV, came back to the sofa with the remote in her hand. "Go and give them a call now, sort something."

Saz got up with, she hoped, not too much enthusiasm and, went to the kitchen to the telephone. "I love you."

"I should hope so. Cup of coffee while you're up, please. Decaf."

While she put on the kettle Saz called Will and then, when they'd agreed on their arrangements, she called Carrie. Carrie wasn't home but Saz left a message and an offer she knew her ex couldn't possibly refuse. Carrie was well behind—as always—with the rent she owed on the flat she sublet (illegally but at the standard council rate) from Saz. Now that she wasn't working herself, Saz had struggled to cover the gap when Carrie was in arrears, Molly taking care of the shortfall. With the certainty of Ross Gallagher's TV wealth behind her, Saz's message offered Carrie not only a temporary rent amnesty, but also some extra cash to go with it. All for occasional on-demand secret babysitting and, more immediately, that Carrie would lie about going out with Saz the next evening. Saz knew Carrie was happy to lie, whether money was attached or not, but somehow she felt marginally less guilty when she made the lie a business transaction. She was more practiced in lies-for-work. She put down the phone feeling like a sneaky sixteen-year-old. And, thinking about the evening she had just planned, realized that was pretty much what she was.

She was about to add boiling water to coffee grounds when she had a better thought and checked the fridge for wine. She went back to Molly. The MMR item was over and her partner sighed in frustration at the half-science she'd just heard from both sides of the argument, then sat up in surprise when Saz kneeled in front of her, full and cold glasses in hand. "I really do love you, Moll."

Molly took the glass. "Looks like it, doesn't it?"

"Shall we drink this and go to bed?"

"Shall we stay here and drink this and not go to bed?"

"Why?"

"Our room is closer to Matilda's. We don't want to disturb her. Not now she's so good with her routine."

"No, we don't."

"No, we don't."

Kiss touch hold. Stop. Kiss hold touch. Reach. Start again. Kiss, kiss more, hold harder, tighter. Kiss, bite. Not kiss, too slow, bite. Stop. Look. Listen. Silent, humming TV, truck rolls past. Smile, giggle, bite, laugh. Kiss again, OK, if you want, there and there and there, lower down, leg feet lips teeth. Hand holding, hand holding flesh. Goose-pimple skin and yes there, you know it, you know it. And again. Push, fast, faster, slow, the flicking quick-step four-step double beat time-step. Wine spilled on sofa and mumbled offers to wash it tomorrow, wine spilled on skin and no offer, dive in, lick it up now. More wine, not spilled, poured this time. Saz's heart beating faster next to Molly's heart, next to Molly's thigh. Saz's heart in her mouth, Molly's sex in her mouth. Same place, know it so well, same moves, again and again and again, so good at this, this so good, but same. Very same. Years of fucking and kissing and coming and going, the years of it, bodies so well matched they simply begin the touch and skin quivers as it knows what comes next, when comes next, who comes next. Saz and Molly moving fluidly and skillfully and a part of Saz's mind watching, noting. Set back, sit back. Sees their abilities, their knowing. Their too-knowing. Sees and wonders and questions and the body is still moving and heart beating a pulsing blood rhythm and yet not all there, not all here, somewhere watching, noticing. Outside. And then the shift. The shift that always comes, the shift that takes the sex from a place of before and certainly again, into now. Just this one. This fuck and only this. Not the many times before or those to come. Just this one time. Two times if you're lucky. Something about her own skin, an attention in her cells, tension in herself. And wait, two three four—release.

Saz curled into Molly's arms, her body cooling against the floor, warm touching Molly, and she wondered how it could be that she could lose her brain so readily. That huge moment between watching herself and feeling odd about being so used to it, their fucking, the tradition of their fucking, as well as feeling bad about the lies this evening, and then the leap into just body. Or maybe it wasn't a leap—it felt more like she was pulled, that picture she used to love in the *Narnia* books, where the painting of the ship just dragged the kids into it, and they felt the ocean spray before they'd even left their bedroom—pulled into a whole new place. How weird that every time, no matter where her head was, once that leap was made, it was as if it hadn't happened countless times before. Saz had never been able to work out if it was her body or Molly's body or the combination of the two that made this possible, the leaving her head behind. But she knew she never wanted to lose it. And she knew that with each step towards her own past, the loss became a more real possibility, the lies distancing her from Molly, the possibility that truth would send Molly from her. She stretched out to better feel her own relaxation, better ignore her fears. Molly threw Asmita's old green travel rug over her partner as she switched off lights and TV, took up glasses, washed dishes. Later, the two women bumbled through teeth cleaning quietly so as not to disturb Matilda, quietly so as not to disturb the skin ease between the two of them. And then they went to bed.

As they fell asleep Molly talked about Ian. Just that evening, laughing at Matilda in the bath, she'd realized how vibrant the images of her daughter were when she was at work and thought of Matilda—her child was always active. And she'd noticed that the store of images she had of her father were gradually becoming static.

"It's as if he's all photos now, Saz. I used to see him, in my head, as if he was doing stuff. In their garden, or playing cards with my ma, holding Matilda when she was tiny. But now all the pictures I have in my head look like photos. He's static, still."

Saz squeezed Molly's hand, pushed away the still images that had come into her own mind. A bright spring morning, a screaming mouth, cold skin, broken bones. Forced herself back here, back now. Running away again. "Yeah, but loads of the pictures in my head are still too. Like most of the ones from when Cassie and I were small. I'm not even sure any of them are real images; I think half my memories are actually the photos Mum and Dad took when we were kids. Maybe none of our memories are true recollections." She could but hope.

Molly frowned. "Yes, but I can picture you yesterday. Making breakfast, shouting at your sister on the phone …"

"We were discussing her husband's birthday party; it just sounded like shouting."

"That's what you two always say. Anyway, I see that picture as a moving one. But all the ones with my dad, they've turned into stills."

"Color?"

"Old-fashioned over-bright technicolor."

"Nice. Maybe it's our generation. We're so used to photo images that it's what our brains do to our own memories, turns them into photos. Puts borders round our people."

Wishing she was right. Wishing the pictures coming into her head could be captured and put away, made safe in albums. Wishing they weren't bleeding black and white back into her own life now. Molly fell asleep searching for moving pictures of her father. Saz drifted—too slowly—away from images of her past where sticks and stones didn't always break bones, but large concrete slabs certainly did.

TWENTY-THREE

Sally left school early that day. As planned. As agreed. As if she wanted to. Maybe she did want to. Coming close to the end of term, classroom hot with tired sighs and the sweating thighs of adolescent potential. She checked the watch she had been given three years ago, glass face scratched with time, birthday present watch, big deal in her family, the thirteenth birthday watch. Her father had one, her sister had one, she had one. It was time. Chair scraped back on wooden floor, one leg missing its rubber stopper and the splintered rut in the floor adjusted its depth once more.

Eyes right, Sally stood up from her seat. Eyes front, Sally walked to the teacher, backed against the blackboard by the uncomprehending faces of his yawning class. Eyes in the back row met and mouths grinned, smiling at what was to come. What was expected and what was to come. This was yet another badly designed classroom where the afternoon sun turned pale spring into tropical warmth, school bags and books exuding over-ripe banana and bruised apple odors, stained breath of a dozen bulimic girls raising an acid ozone to the fluorescent ceiling. Sally felt eager encouragement at her back as she whispered period and surprise and can I go now, please, whispered it to the young man just out of training college, just loud enough for the front row to hear and enjoy his discomfort. He blushed, Sally didn't, she left. The room, the building, the grounds. Safe on the streets, safer on the streets by far than in the crowded corridors she was leaving behind.

Sally walked up the road, round the corner, past the sweet shop, owner and her son gearing up for the post-school shoplifting rush and then the chemist, lazy posters peeling in the hot glass windows. She side-stepped the betting shop, its doorway cluttered with ever-hopeful old men and their littered potential. Sally took one back street and then another. Past a second parade of shops, a third row of ugly Edwardian houses, their red brick too red, imposing facades too heavy. Sally hated the suburbs, this one in particular, hated living out here in no-man's land. No-woman's land. It would have been much faster to walk home direct. Sally was not going home.

She stopped at her designated resting place, against the wall, partially hidden by an old willow, waiting, and talked herself through her script. And it was a script, those words she was planning to say, the words the others had coached her in saying. She'd realized this morning that it was a script, while she listened to Will reading aloud his allotted three pages of *Macbeth,* reading out loud in Miss Taylor's English class. A-level required syllabus and just Will Gallagher in the whole group who had not only read the play once at home, but was happy to read it aloud again, to the whole room. No one took the piss when Will was reading, he was good at it. Will Gallagher was many things, but he was not shy. Andrea Browne said that Miss Taylor fancied him, had seen the way the teacher looked at her boyfriend. She was probably right, everyone fancied Will Gallagher. Even when he was showing off, maybe especially then. And listening to him in Miss Taylor's class this morning, Sally had realized, warm and sweating a little in her nylon-cotton mix school blouse, that the job she was doing this afternoon was acting as well. The words they had all encouraged her to say were her script.

Sally wished she were as confident as Will now. Wished she were as smart and eager for attention as Daniel. Either attribute would work. Skill or aggressive self-belief. Sally knew herself well enough to understand that the agitation she was feeling here, waiting, worrying, was because she was too aware of what happened next. Daniel wouldn't think about it as long as people noticed him and Will wouldn't give a fuck either way, if the plan worked out in the end. She shouldn't think about it. Should just do it. Would just do it. Heard the faint school bell four streets away. One long ring and then a second short note. Pictured kids standing up, slamming desks, teachers trying to shout out homework and end-of-lesson wrap-ups, drowned out in scraping chairs and drumming, running feet. Sally checked her birthday watch. Waiting. Sun shining. Just do it.

Five minutes more and Janine Marsden came running down the road.

Always leaving her classes as quickly as possible, out of the room and out of the building as quickly as she could, running fast to the safety of her home. Mother and father both at work, little brother out, and a couple of hours where Janine could have time to herself, just be herself. Hide. Sally was hidden. And then revealed.

"Hi, Janine."

TWENTY-FOUR

When Saz walked into the early evening pub it was already smoky and noisy, midnight colors in a seven o'clock room. It made sense that Daniel would come to a place like this with Becky. In the dim lighting the girl would easily pass for at least eighteen, and the building was too far away from the sixth form college and much too traditional for any but the most indifferent of fellow students or teachers to be there. It was a drinking pub, not a style bar.

Daniel Carver was waiting for her. And so was Becky. A big fat I-told-you-so grin on her face, she stroked Daniel's arm as Saz approached his table and then stood up, smiling, "I'll just be in the Ladies. If you want me." The first directed at Saz, the latter at Daniel.

The two adults eyed each other, half their lives falling away between them. Saz noted that the man seated before her was still tall, lanky; even after all this time he hadn't really filled out. He looked at her thoughtfully assembled dress, well-cut hair, understated but useful makeup, the not-quite-so-narrow hips of her woman's body. She was too old for him.

Daniel spoke first. "Sally?"

"Saz. Daniel?"

"Yeah. Some people go for Dan. I'll answer to anything but Danny. No change. I always think name-changers must have something to hide, don't you? Saz?"

"Maybe."

"So, can I get you a drink?"

"No. Thanks. Will's outside. Will Gallagher. We need to talk to you."

"What? Our Will? Is that what this is about? Ross Gallagher off the telly?"

Oddly, despite his surprise that Saz was not alone, she had a sense that Daniel was enjoying this. Maybe because the pub was his territory, or perhaps he was already buoyed up with Becky's account of yesterday's meeting, knowing Saz would arrive at some point, and knowing she'd been hoping to surprise him—either way, he certainly wasn't as disturbed at the thought of seeing Will as Saz had been. Maybe it was a lad thing, the potential re-ignition of their bloke-bonding. Or maybe it was just good old-fashioned star-fucking. Whatever, Saz knew Becky wouldn't leave them all that long, no matter how important her perfect lip-line was, and she needed to get in quick with her story.

"There's some old school reunion I haven't been told about?"

"Yeah, kind of. Janine Marsden has been in touch. With Will."

Daniel looked down at his near-empty pint, back up at Saz. His eyes were dark; he was no longer smiling.

"Fuck. You're kidding?"

Saz shook her head, pleased to have shocked him out of his ease. "Wish I was. She's been calling Will. She wants to see us. All five of us."

"She what?"

"That's what she told Will. In one of her letters, or calls, I don't know all the details. Can't say I wanted to know anything about it when he first told me. But we do need to do something. She wants to meet up with all of us."

"Can't we just tell her to fuck off?"

"And chance her calling the papers? Contacting our families? That's what she's threatening. You really want to risk having all that brought up again?"

The door to the Ladies opened and Becky began to make her way across the smoky room, Saz spoke fast. "Will's outside in the car; he's booked a table, somewhere quiet so we can talk. We do need to talk."

"Yeah. Sure."

"And you can't bring the girl."

Daniel was all compliance and forced calm, Becky close enough for Saz to smell her body-spray perfume. Aerosol musk—just as brutal as it had been back when Saz and Andrea had smothered their own bodies in it.

"No. Right. Look, give me a minute to get rid of Becky. You're outside?"

"Two streets up, on the right. And it would be useful if she didn't see Will."

"Yeah. No problem." Daniel was already checking his pocket for his wallet, gathering coins from the table.

Saz was walking away just as Becky was about to slide into the chair beside Daniel, the teenager arriving in time to realize there would be no more opportunities this evening to further emphasize her barrier-breaking relationship with the teacher, though she took his head in her hands and pulled his bald spot between her enhanced breasts nonetheless. While Becky liked an audience, she didn't always demand one. Daniel generally fulfilled the role perfectly adequately—mentor and acolyte, all rolled into one substantial fuck. Which meant she was very unhappy when he explained he intended to follow Saz and leave her behind. Though not before he'd bought her a double vodka. And another pack of Marlboro Lights. And promised her a bloody good party on Sunday afternoon. The barman watched as she blew Daniel's departing back a blow-job kiss. She'd sent three text messages before the door slammed shut, twilight and fresh air left waiting on the step.

Daniel climbed into the back seat and Will started the car.

"Well, this is lovely, all together again. So what the fuck's going on?"

As he drove off, Will Gallagher eyed Daniel in the rear-view mirror, the reflection offering him Daniel's worried face.

"Let's catch up a little first."

Daniel shrugged, "Nice to see you're still in charge of the conversation, Will."

"If I can be. Been seeing the girl long?"

Daniel nodded, "Few months officially. Since I left the school at the end of last term."

"Very wise. I expect she's grateful to you, taking a special interest in her education and all."

The men smiled at each other, and started on a discussion of younger women, the ones they so would, until Saz interjected, "For fuck's sake, of course Becky thinks she's doing something exciting, he was a teacher at her school—sorry, college—she's breaking rules, being a rebel. But bloody hell, Daniel, what on earth do you have to talk about?"

"You, actually. Yesterday evening Becky told me all about you."

"All that she knew."

"More than I did. What do you reckon, Will? Our little Sally a lezz?"

Will patted Saz's knee beside him. "Molly's little Sally now actually, Daniel."

"So there is a lady friend?"

"They've got a daughter as well. Very happy family set-up from what I saw."

Daniel turned to Saz. "And my mum always said she thought the lezz thing was a phase you'd grow out of."

Saz laughed, "Yeah, well, your mum always was a rubbish judge of character. She thought you were perfect."

Will sighed. "How very like old times this is. And how very dull. Shut up now, children, and let Daddy tell you what we're doing this evening, because you know what? There are far more pressing matters than which one of you has the smarter mouth or the higher moral ground."

They walked into the restaurant and Will took charge as always, ordering a shared meal for the three of them and, when the waiter had left, Daniel leaned forward, his voice lower now, lad-banter all gone. "So, what's the story? Is she for real?"

"Janine Marsden?" Will was quiet now too. "Unfortunately I think she is."

"What does she want?"

"Like we said in the car, she wants to see us."

"Us?"

"You, me, Sally, Andrea, and Ewan."

"She actually said that? Named all of us? Ewan too?"

Daniel looked from Will to Saz. Saz shrugged, nodded at Will. "I don't think he's making it up. What would be the point?"

Daniel reached for his wine glass. "No, I guess not. Fancy that. After all this time she finally did it."

"What do you mean?" Saz asked, flushing hot and scared, glad of the low lighting.

Daniel took a mouthful of wine, swallowed it without tasting, "You know, found us. Got back to us. Still, arranging a meeting's going to be tricky."

"No kidding." Will shook his head.

Daniel smiled, "At least we know how to get hold of Andy."

Saz spoke first. "No?"

"OK then, I know how to get hold of Andy. She lives over near Bristol."

"Doing what?"

"Praying."

"On whom?" Will moved his glass so the waiter could put down another plate, and grinned at his own joke.

Saz wasn't laughing, "Praying?"

"For my lost soul last I heard. My mum—source of all wisdom, as we've established—met her Aunty Jane a year or so back. You remember, Will, that Jane we used to really fancy, Andy's dad's little sister? Way younger than all the parents?"

"Big tits, tight jeans, very fine arse?"

"That's the one."

"Oh yeah, I liked her. Didn't you too, Sally?"

"I barely remember the woman," Saz lied. "Can we get on with the matter in hand, please?"

"Do go on." Will waved his hand and Daniel smiled acceptance.

"OK, I knew Andy had got married just after university, some bloke from her course, and they had a couple of kids, fairly young they must have been, but then according to what Aunty Jane told my mum, about five years ago both Andrea's parents died."

"Together?" Saz was listening hard, her own recent grief stirring up unexpected sympathies for the woman she still thought of as a whip-tongued teenager, her company to be enjoyed, but also feared, certainly not someone to be pitied. A woman who had once been so important to her and now, she was quickly realizing, about whom she knew virtually nothing.

"Nope. Mrs. Browne died first. It was all really gruesome according to her Aunty Jane. And then Andy's dad died about six months later.

Broken heart they reckon, he just didn't want to keep going without her."

Will looked up from the food he'd been steadily eating. Protein only. "So grief turned our wild child into a born-again believer? How trite of her."

Saz shook her head, "Andrea was never really a wild child. Part of her was always gagging to settle down, play house."

"Yeah, and quite a lot of her was exactly the opposite," Will said.

"True, but it's hard to hold *Little House on the Prairie* and *Barbarella* together for long. She was going to have to choose one or the other eventually. Maybe that's why she's gone for religion, to handle the contradiction?"

"Or ignore it. So she's really found Jesus?"

Daniel grinned, clearly enjoying his role of informer. "Not exactly, she found Bob."

"The builder?"

"The Buddha."

"What?"

Will was speaking with his mouth full, Saz wasn't hungry. Daniel was well into the story.

"According to Aunty Jane, Andrea left her husband with their two kids, gave up a pretty good career in advertising, and followed this Bob—who just happened to work in the same city firm as her husband, same team what's more—off to his tent or shack or farm, whatever-the-fuck-it-is, halfway up the River Severn. A year later she comes back to get the kids, heartbroken hubby hands them over without a fight. Poor bugger."

Will was bored, he'd never liked Daniel's long stories when they were younger and didn't seem any more interested now. "Daniel, get to the point? If you possibly can?"

Daniel continued, slowly, enjoying Will's irritation. "Well, apparently Andrea and the new bloke now live in splendid isolation, all the while praying for the likes of us. Some Eastern thing my mum thought. Buddhist. Krishna maybe. Though for all I know, they could be Plymouth Brethren, my mum's grasp of comparative theology always was very shaky."

"But you said you know how to get hold of her?" Saz asked.

Daniel took a mouthful of steak from Will's plate. "That's right. See, the lovely Aunty Jane gave Andy my mum's address. They've been exchanging Christmas cards ever since." He looked up across the table. "Andy always signs them to say she's praying for all of us, her little group of best mates from school. Seems to think we might need it."

The men were certain that Andrea would rather hear from Saz than from either of them. Daniel refused to be the bearer of bad news—both Saz and Will recognized his brave mouth and fearful actions from their past. And Will said he would call her—but that he didn't think he could keep her on the line long enough to explain what was going on.

"I doubt very much she's any fonder of me now than when I last dumped her."

"Last dumped her?"

Will smiled at Saz. "You know how dim some girls can be. Won't take telling just the once, very persistent. You have to dump them from a great height to get through to them. She said she never wanted to speak to me again. Only not quite so nicely."

Daniel nodded. "Gallagher charm in action, how I've missed learning from the master. No wonder Andy ended up with two husbands when you were her perfect first. Or maybe she just can't decide who to stay with because it's really you she still loves, always has done, all this time?"

"Very willing to help, Daniel. Any time you need tips, you only have to ask."

"Yeah. Right. Didn't I read something about that producer you were shagging last year? That one who dumped you and then sold her story to the *Sun*?"

"She wasn't a producer, she was a runner. And she didn't dump me, I dumped her when I realized she was too young for me. Nineteen, Daniel, too young. It didn't look good. I can give you her number though, if you fancy trading up to an adult model any time? She's probably nearly twenty by now?"

The arrival of another bottle of wine called a halt to the men's sparring. Even Daniel knew better than to draw the waiter's attention to Will's public persona while they were still discussing their collective past. Saz agreed to be the first point of contact with Andrea, though said she'd have to sort out a few babysitting problems first. She didn't explain her reasoning for wanting to keep Molly out of what was going on, and neither of the men asked. The desire to keep past and present apart was perfectly understandable to all of them. Caught in a shiver of her own fears, Saz figured the men felt as sick as she did. The danger posed to Will's career was obvious—the nation might love a charming bastard on its screens, happily believe that every passionate woman really did crave a bit of rough with a golden heart—it didn't like the same story so much when it took up tabloid covers as revealed truth. For Saz it was easier to see the whole thing as Will's problem; it meant she didn't have to look too far back to her own involvement. After the initial explanation of what was going on, and agreement on a plan of action, Janine Marsden's name was not mentioned again. Instead the three of them settled into their old pattern—men-as-boys ganging up against Saz, Saz and Daniel taking the piss out of Will's new fame and new name, Saz and Will mocking Daniel's still-present *auteur* aspirations. All of it too close and too true, but easy as well. While each of them was nervy about the news from Janine Marsden, they were also used to being with each other. They had lived through some of their most important moments together. It was irrelevant that not one of them ever acknowledged that time in their current lives if they could help it. They were bound, and they knew it.

As Saz drove away she thought about herself and the two men all those years ago. That time and place so long ago when she had both craved and despised their company, loved being part of the group and loathed herself for loving it, for the compromises she made to keep her place. In and out, just as she'd always known herself to be. She arrived home late and very sober. Molly and Matilda were sleeping together in the big bed. Saz lifted her daughter and laid her carefully in her cot, lifted her partner and laid her carefully in her arms. Around three in the morning Matilda started crying and Saz went to their baby. Held her, soothed her, lullabied her back to sleep. Molly woke when Saz climbed carefully back into bed, Molly turned in Saz's arms, her partner her passion and her pillow. Saz turned in on herself, in another place, kissing another face.

TWENTY-FIVE

We were nine when we first played "kissing." We weren't best friends, I didn't have best friends, but that year we sat together in Mrs. King's class and a few times we slept over at each other's houses. No spare beds at her place or mine, but it wasn't strange to share a bed, not then. Top and tail, head to foot. Turn in the night face to face, lips to lips, mouth to mouth. And more. Turn in the night, but never in the day. In public. We knew to be quiet, not to enjoy ourselves too loudly. We knew it was enjoyable. And we knew part of the fun was the secret. We knew too—I don't know how we knew, we were so young, stupid and naive in so many ways—but we did—we knew it wouldn't be OK. That the boys and girls playing doctors and nurses at school got in trouble when they were found out. Had to go and speak to the Deputy Head, one at a time, into the big office, embarrassed and denying and leaving crying. If doctors and nurses was so wrong, we knew there'd be a problem with nurses and nurses. We didn't know any men nurses then, and only one lady doctor.

So we didn't tell. This was our secret. And we perfected it, that year we were friends, we got good at it. Very good. And then she decided it was done, too much, over. We were too old to play kissing, she said. I didn't mind dropping the play part. And I didn't believe her either, I thought we were probably just old enough. But we did stop. Because we had to. Because it was safer that way. Because she wasn't my best friend and not even my good friend; then she wasn't my friend at all.

I always thought she'd come back though.

TWENTY-SIX

The woman who came to meet Saz from the train didn't look like an anti-establishment, eastern mystic. Or a born-again hippy. Or any of the things Andrea's Aunty Jane had assured Daniel's mother she would. She looked like a nice middle-class mother. New jeans, bright green trainers, ironed pale green shirt, and a denim jacket hung over one arm, two carefully dressed children hanging on to her arms, the boy in jeans and sweatshirt, the girl in a little denim dress. But Saz knew only too well appearances could be deceptive. She knew that in a recent *Your-TV* poll, the man most British grandparents wanted to see their granddaughter walking up the aisle towards was Ross Gallagher. She knew that Daniel Carver, with his tall, thin body and bald patch and staffroom-straight clothes didn't look much like the kind of teacher to be having an affair with one of his more advanced ex-students. She knew that she and Molly hadn't looked a great deal like the other couples at their ante-natal classes. And she also knew that, unless Andrea had totally changed personality, the perfect Boden mother she now showed herself to be was not necessarily all there was to know.

Saz allowed herself to be drawn into Andrea's delicate hug. Andrea smelt of good perfume and thin sunshine on fresh cotton, was taller than her still, and her short-cut hair was just graying at the temples—a sight which both pleased and disturbed Saz. Something to do with knowing her own hair hadn't yet started on that route, while noting that, after all this time, Andrea still seemed more adult than she did. The woman who'd come to meet her had no trouble conveying an air of ease. Perhaps it was because she was on her own territory, Andrea had been very clear on the phone that Saz had to come to see her and not vice versa. Saz hoped the confidence wasn't to do with whatever practice Andrea had adopted; those of abundant faith too often wanted to share it round, and Saz was perfectly happy to skip her turn. With any luck there wouldn't be quite enough time to attempt her conversion today—Saz had three hours before the return train, with just enough time on both stuttering train journeys to drink several cups of bad coffee while berating herself as an appalling mother and a wicked partner.

Andrea led her across the carpark to a large and shiny people carrier. Up close, Andrea's immaculate mother image was even clearer—smooth tan, light makeup, no jewelry other than a plain white gold wedding band topped with a subtle diamond on her ring finger. The presence of the two children in the car stopped Saz asking about Janine straightaway and so she questioned the country life instead.

"I thought you ... I mean, Daniel's mother told him that you were ..."

"Living in a field? A tent? An ashram?"

"I don't think Mrs. Carver knows what an ashram is."

"Probably not. Well, we were, sort of."

"But you're not now?"

Andrea pulled out of the carpark as she explained. "Robert and I started at this farm out here. He'd been working in the city, I was in advertising, fairly successful too, but after a while we just got sick of it. We were working all hours, never seeing each other, no time for the children—we have three now."

Saz nodded, taking it in. Molly always said that of the parents who came into the hospital, the more kids they had, the more they figured they knew what they were doing—whether they were right or not. Andrea certainly looked self-confident, though that could just have been to do with wealth; it was a very big car. However, unlike the parents who blocked up her road dropping off just one child from their eight-person vehicle every morning, Saz figured that with a family of five, this didn't quite count as a Selfishly Unnecessary Vehicle. She forced herself to listen more carefully.

"I wanted somewhere we could use our old skills, but also learn new ones. Robert was keen to be around the children more, then we heard about the place out here. We stuck with community life for a couple of years, but it wasn't really us."

"So you moved out?"

"We're happier as a smaller unit. We have a little farm of our own now."

Saz looked around her at the spotlessly clean, clearly very new vehicle. "Doing well?"

"Not as well as we'd hoped, not yet. Organic vegetables, free range eggs, a few specialist flowers. We did expect more business from the London exiles in the other villages round here, but maybe it just takes time. No," she said, patting the steering wheel, "this isn't from the farm. Robert's grandfather died recently. And we bought two new cars."

"Well, that's lucky, if you needed the help." Saz wondered if that was all the family death had meant to them, more money.

Andrea smiled. "We think so." She turned the car into a narrow opening in a hedgerow, took a quick right and pulled up outside an imposing Edwardian farmhouse.

"Well, here we are. Welcome home, Sally."

"It's Saz now."

"Yes, I heard you say so on the phone. Since when?"

"Since I left school, left home. My mum always called me Sarah, still does, but everyone else knows me as Saz. It's who I am."

Andrea's grin took Saz back years. "You really have run away from your past, haven't you?"

Saz felt her anger rising, that Andrea was trying to push her into a place where she always came out better than Saz did. Saz hadn't liked it back then, and she really didn't like it now. She took a slow breath and slipped down to the gravel driveway, working hard to speak softly in front of the children.

"I still live in London. I visit my mum and dad, my sister and her family regularly. I often go back to where we all came from. I drive past that school, down those streets, at least once a fortnight, if not more often since my own daughter was born. How about you, Andrea? How often do you go back?"

Andrea just looked at her for a while, then she shrugged. "Well, things change, don't they?"

"Yeah, they do."

Saz followed the children and Andrea into the house. Wishing Molly beside her, Matilda in her arms, wishing herself far away and safe at home. Safe in her easy normal usual incredibly bloody ordinary life. She closed the door behind her, cursing Will and Daniel for sending her out here alone.

The happy couple insisted on showing her around their gorgeous home—it really was massive and even while Saz fought to keep her spare-room jealousy in check, she managed to make at least some of the right noises, still doing her best to scour the place for anything that might give her a better clue as to Andrea's current state of mind. When they'd completed a circuit of the house, they went back downstairs to the big old kitchen. Andrea made coffee, the third child appeared airing a cut finger and a new, blood-glazed painting to pin on the wall, and Robert produced fresh bread with fat slices of his home-cured ham, organic plum jam tarts for the kids. Saz quite fancied a tart herself, but was wary enough of Andrea to know this was one time she really needed to prove her adult credentials, not express her youthful *joie de vivre* by exhibiting her childish desires—a shame, because the tarts looked really good.

As soon as Robert had left the room with the children, Saz leaped in. "We have to talk about Janine. Can we make an excuse to go off somewhere together?" Andrea looked at Saz and smiled, said nothing. Saz tried really hard to resist the urge to slap her. "It's just that I assume you don't want Robert to know about Janine? Daniel and Will seem very keen to keep it all quiet."

"They would. Will's career-driven, and Daniel ... well, unless he's changed a great deal, he's probably still very ambitious himself, isn't he?"

"Ambitious and bitter probably. But would you be OK with Robert knowing about Janine?"

"Robert understands that I was not always as careful of other people as I am now," Andrea said.

"That's not quite what I said."

Andrea didn't answer, just continued to smile.

Saz stared, then asked, "Does Robert know about Ewan?"

Andrea shook her head, speaking quietly. "I told him that we had a little … gang. After you called I explained that someone is trying to blackmail Will about something he did as a young man. As a child really."

"Something he did? Just Will?"

Andrea ignored her. "And that if we agree to meet with this woman, she'll drop it. That's more than enough for Robert to know, don't you think?"

"And are you going to come?"

"I don't know … it all seems so long ago now."

"Not so long ago that Janine's forgotten, and Will said she insisted on having all five of us there."

Andrea laughed, "That's going to be a bit tricky, isn't it?"

"It's not funny, it's serious, for all of us."

"Why? Do you have nasty little secrets as well, Sally?"

"Bloody hell, Andrea, don't you? Isn't that why you haven't told your husband the whole story?"

Andrea put the coffee mug down on the table and, just as Robert came back into the kitchen, hissed at Saz, "Why the fuck would I?"

And then, with more coffee poured and jam tarts finally passed round to the adults, Robert began. He was clearly a man used to being listened to. There was the unsatisfying life of a rich man and a wealthy woman, the lack of truth in city work, the constant stress, that awful daily train trip. Though Robert was keen to underline the soul-searching nature of their conversion as well— this was about the inner journey as much as the outer. Besides that, Andrea admitted, interrupting Robert briefly, there was nothing about her soul's yearning that involved mucking out pigs. Saz was relieved to see in Andrea's disdain for dirt the sharp-tongued girl of their teens. The girl whose nails were always pink-painted, and who would never have left a city apartment for the country life, even if it had an indoor-outdoor swimming pool attached.

Andrea went on to confess how bad they felt about their affair. They knew at the time that it was wrong, but anyway, and because this was where their hearts and souls had led them, they had to be together. This much Saz already knew, but apparently they needed to tell her in their own way. Their truth. As opposed, she imagined, to Andrea's ex-husband's truth—the one about love being a choice, and passion being an option, and even a first marriage being a commitment. She thought all this and said none of it. Because she knew everyone used the same excuses, and who was she to call Robert and Andrea on it when she'd used those excuses herself? Although she'd never thought about blaming a higher power, as Robert was now doing.

"Andrea and I were destined to make a difference, together. The kind of difference you too could make, Sally ..."

"Saz."

"If only you'd turn your heart over to the greater good."

"Give and you shall receive," Andrea intoned, nodding her head as if she'd just thought of a really clever new thing. "It's all about surrender—of the ego and the ties that bind us to the material world."

Saz really had been trying to hold it in, but this was excessive. "But you've got so much—three cars outside! What are you talking about?"

Robert smiled down at her and Saz wanted to punch him. "We earned these benefits through prayer and hard work. And now our life is truly comfortable."

Andrea grinned, "Which leaves us more space for prayer." Saz sighed. She could have tried harder. Asked about the starving millions, where they fitted in with this great plan that simple prayer granted, everything from a life partner to a three-speed ice-cream maker. Could have suggested that the world was full of people who had faith and worked hard, they just didn't all have a rich family to leave them a deathbed start-up kit. Could even have asked what happened to Andrea's wild side. Was it truly possible to deny that in some part of her she still craved excitement and danger and thrills? But she simply couldn't be bothered. Two of the three children had started a mini-war in the next room, the toddler was screaming upstairs, and all these two in front of her wanted to do was spout platitudes about belief.

And as yet they hadn't even got around to telling Saz what exactly it was they did believe in. For all she knew it was the full pantheon of Greek, Roman, and Norse gods lifting them to this astonishing degree of self-satisfaction. She was bored. And her train was going in an hour. She excused herself and went upstairs to the toilet— the downstairs one had two children in it, fighting to see who could block it first. When she came back downstairs she felt calmer and more certain than she'd been since meeting Andrea at the station.

"Look, I need go soon. Quite obviously, you have a lovely home and no doubt a lovely life and if those kids manage to survive the next half hour without ripping each other's arms off, I'm sure they'll grow up to be lovely people. But I live in a different world and I'm bringing up my child in a different world."

"You mean the real world, Sally? All worlds are as real as we make them."

Saz wasn't to be stalled. She ignored the smiling Robert and concentrated on Andrea. "You said Robert knows all about you, about your past. In that case he also knows that between us, we fucked up pretty badly back then. And right now, Will and Daniel are waiting to hear if you'll help us sort out a mess that all of us created and each of us has, in our own way, run away from." Neither of them responded, so she continued, "While it might seem strange to you that, after all this time, Will needs your help, he does. We all do. I've done what you asked, I've come out here, listened to the pair of you, now it's time to go. I don't want to miss my train, so I need to know if you're going to be part of this or not. Well, Andrea?"

Robert took Andrea's hand and then the two of them each reached out a hand to Saz.

"I don't ..."

Robert's hand was big, and surprisingly soft, he squeezed Saz's fingers and spoke quietly. "We're asking the inner voice to guide us."

"The what?"

Andrea's hand was small, and cold, as it always had been, finely shaped nails carefully shaded, she pinched Saz's fingers hard between her own, turned to whisper, "If you'd shut up, Sally, maybe just for a minute, you might even hear it yourself."

115

They held hands then, over the table. Saz stood, staring around the room, eager to get away. Andrea was so clearly exactly the same woman she'd been years ago and yet somehow she'd forced herself into this pastel-shaded mold, husband and kids and house and money, all straight out of the catalogs they'd spent teenage years despising and envying in equal measure. This was one half of Andrea only, taken over and made the whole—Andrea out of focus, and the fuzziness was disorienting. Saz swayed between the two of them. Then the breadmaker stopped its noise. The children were distracted by a fox on the lawn. They ran outside and their noise level fell as quickly as it had risen. It certainly wasn't a voice she heard, but Saz understood in a rush that she'd been here before now. Many times, desperate to run away, get past the uncomfortable place and back to where she was safe. Only this time she wasn't running from, she was running to. She knew Andrea would agree to meet with Janine Marsden. Just like the rest of them, she had her secrets, no matter what she said about Robert. She really had no choice. Saz was scared about the meeting to come and running full speed at it anyway.

Andrea drove her back to the station and they agreed that Saz would call when they had a time to meet with the others.

As Saz climbed down from the vehicle, Andrea turned to her, "I know you think it's strange, but this is my life now."

"What about the Andrea who loved to fuck and take drugs and drink and party all hours?"

"She grew up."

"And away?"

"Not entirely. I replaced her with other stuff."

"Like your faith?"

Andrea shook her head. "No, not really. I mean, I do believe, but that's more Robert's thing actually."

Saz was confused, "But you said …"

"I go along with it. It works for him and that means it works for me too. I left one husband already, Sally, I have three children. I might crave excitement, but I crave stability more. Always have done. Even with all the problems it caused, being part of our little gang back then was a safety net for me. I want a normal life, I don't want to have to try hard again. It was hard enough leaving Tim when I fell in love with Robert. I'm sure you think I'm weak, but I don't believe I'm unusual. Most people I know would choose safety over the alternative. The truth is, it matters to me that my life looks good, acceptable, from the outside."

"Even if you're not truly happy with it on the inside?"

Andrea started the engine again, frowning. "Truly happy? That's asking a lot, don't you think?" She nodded towards the station entrance. "You should go. You don't want to miss your train."

In the train Saz pulled a thin strip of photos from the back of her jeans. It was what she'd been looking for when she went upstairs to the loo. She'd checked out the possible places that any secrets might be hidden when Andrea and Robert were showing her the glories of their beautiful home. No matter what Andrea said, Saz didn't believe that her old friend was entirely capable of settling down, giving up completely on true happiness—or its attendant dangers. Aware that the children had commandeered the downstairs toilet, Saz had taken her only chance and headed straight for the happy couple's bedroom. On Andrea's bedside table was a pile of books, mostly obscuring a large silver-framed photo of her and Robert's wedding. Saz was fifteen when Andrea had shown off the perfect hiding place in her little lilac bedroom. Her good Catholic parents would have been furious if they'd known she was on the pill. Andrea had invented the perfect safe. Every morning she took off the back of the photo frame, removed the stabilizing piece of cardboard, took her pill, and put the frame back together again. The frame that held her dead grandma's picture was deep; it had stored the pills, up to three grams of speed, as well as photos of Andrea and Will in compromising positions.

Saz wasn't sure what she was looking for when she carefully took apart the frame, but she knew there had to be something; she didn't believe anyone could change that much. When she pulled out the photo, she knew she'd found it. She'd stuffed it down the back of her jeans, put the frame back together, and hurried down-stairs. She waited until the train was well away from the station before taking a good long look. Staring up at her were Andrea and Daniel—the adult versions, fairly recent versions—in four full-color photo-booth poses. They did not look like just good friends.

TWENTY-SEVEN

Time to make it happen.

Sally walked back with Janine to her home, saying they needed to talk, she knew things were hard, she wanted to make it better. Said how she'd been thinking about it too. Talked to her sister Cassie, you know how sisters are good at this stuff? Janine didn't. Sally knew Janine didn't, but it was a thing to say, a name to use. Janine's big brother was in the army now, her little brother drove her crazy, she didn't say much to her mother, and she barely conversed with her father. Not because he wasn't nice, but who talked to their dad? She was sixteen, what was there for the two of them to say? Sally nodded, agreed, carried on. Her thought was that the boys—Will Gallagher for one, and Daniel Carver for two—they just needed to get to know Janine better, they all did, all the others. Because Andrea Browne wasn't really like that, her whole school image, she wasn't that bitchy at all, not once you got to know her. And sure, Will was preoccupied with how bloody gorgeous he thought he was, and Daniel was just too fucking clever, but there was more to them than that. More to all of them. (Sally was lying, doing it well, surprising herself and believing her story more with every scripted word.) And Sally had a plan. She was sick of all the stuff that was going on every day, and if she was sick of it, then Janine must be really fed up. So maybe there was a way to fix things. Maybe, if they just had a talk. Got to know each other a bit better.

Janine stared. She and Sally had been friends years ago. Not great friends, best friends, but there was that time, those times, way back, when they'd known each other better. Sat together in

119

primary school, surnames one after the other in the register and became friends out of proximity if nothing else. That had been before big school, before the move up and away, on to new people. Before Sally moved on to new people. Janine shook her head, screwed up her forehead, that annoying wincing thing she did that had always pissed people off, always got her picked on. Sally tried not to notice it, not to comment, asked Janine if she thought maybe they could try. Janine tried a laugh, thought perhaps Sally was offering up the possibility of friendship as a new joke at her expense. But then Sally smiled back. Not a teasing, taunting smile, but a real one. A smile Janine recognized and remembered, from way back, when it was nice. Apparently Sally meant what she was saying, meant they could make it better. And so Janine agreed. How could she not? She'd had enough of the fear and the sickness in her gut every morning.

"Yeah, maybe we could."

"OK, do you want to come back to mine?"

But Janine had to get the dinner on, her dad was working late, doing an extra shift for his mate. Her little brother went to judo on Thursdays. Her mum would be home late too; on Thursdays she picked up the shopping on her way home from work, a tube of Smarties at the bottom of her bag for Janine, Twix for Sam. So there was no one at home right then, she had to get the tea on for them all. Sally knew all this, had expected all this, told the others all this.

"No, I can't, I have to get back." Janine automatically walking on, Janine who didn't know how to trust this surprising new possibility but was also so pleasured by the hope of reprieve that she was eager to make a leap of faith, wanted to believe. To make friends. Have friends. Be friends. Again. Sally was wondering what to say next, how to make it happen, how to get Janine back, and then Janine turned round.

"But you could come to mine? If you like." Even as she made the offer Janine felt her stomach lurch. Again the self-doubt, back-sliding, knowing only too well that eagerness had so often been her downfall, a spur for the nasty barbs, an opening through which they hurled their little hurts. Each new thought tumbling out on top of the other one, each new thought squirming past averted eyes, heavy frown, and then the rest of Janine Marsden's offer mumbled between tight lips: "I mean, only if you want to. It's not far."

Sally knew it wasn't far. That was why she was standing there, on the way to Janine's house, in the opposite direction from her own home. Why she'd left school early, to get here on time. She knew where Janine lived. "Yeah. OK. Let's go."

Janine's house was poor. Sally's house wasn't flash either, but there was a difference. Both her parents worked, not bad jobs and they got by OK. This was more like properly poor. Sally didn't know what had happened. When they were little kids the Marsdens had had a bigger house, much nicer, way nicer than Sally's. But the year after they moved up to big school, something had happened and Janine's dad had lost a bunch of money and they had to move house and her dad went to hospital and when he came back he had to get another job and her mum started going to work too and everything was different. Where Janine lived now was more like Will's dad's place. Will Gallagher had got some kind of scholarship to be at their school, as well as the exams they'd all had to do. Everyone knew Will's dad didn't have any money, but the rest of them had long since stopped taking the piss about it. Will didn't have a mother at home, she'd buggered off years ago according to Andy. That was why Will was so nasty about the girls who fucked around on the blokes they went out with, why he'd never two-timed anyone, said he never would either. Will thought fucking around on your boyfriend or girlfriend was disgusting behavior. Andy told Sally that Will thought lying was the worst thing ever. Andy told Sally that Will was just really hurt by his mum leaving. And that it explained a lot.

Will didn't talk about his mum, he just got on, living with his dad, the two of them, blokes together really, in this flat above the old sweetshop in their road. But Will's was a different kind of poor to Janine's, it looked the same, but it felt different. Maybe because it wasn't what they were used to, maybe the Marsdens still weren't used to it. Sally understood gradations of poor. Understood a few gradations of rich as well, knew they weren't all the same. Sally understood she was right in the middle when it came to her own mates, but if you included all the other kids she knew, the whole school say, then she and Will and Janine Marsden were mostly kind of closer to the poor end. Not crappy poor, but not like most of the kids at their school either.

Daniel's place was pretty much like Sally's, except there was his film equipment all over the place—he was an only child and his mum really spoilt him and let him have whatever he wanted like that. Sally's mum thought it was stupid of Mrs. Carver, but Sally wouldn't have minded her mum being a bit stupid like that sometimes. Ewan's place was different though—it was a house and surgery all in the same big new house, modern and low. His dad was a doctor, and Ewan's mother was the practice nurse. Everyone knew doctors earned loads of money, so the Stirlings had some nicer things, a bit bigger house, but they weren't as flash as Sally had expected before she got to know Ewan. He was going to be a doctor too. But not just a GP like his father, as Will said, lancing old men's boils and kids with snotty noses and your hand up and down smelly cunts all day, definitely not. Ewan was aiming way higher than that, he was going to be a surgeon. Loads more money in surgery. Plastic surgeon maybe. Treating beautiful people all day and just making them more beautiful. And Ewan was clever too, really good at chemistry and biology, so that helped.

Ewan wanted to have money, he liked the idea of being rich, richer than his mum and dad anyway. He wanted to be rich like Andrea Browne's parents. Mr Browne did something with money, some banking thing, no one understood what really, but it meant that at her fifteenth birthday party they had waiters handing out food on trays. Andrea said it was embarrassing actually, and all they had to drink was disgusting wine and no cider or even any beers. Sally had thought it was cool, waiters for wine and little canapés on trays, but she didn't say so. Sally didn't say much when it involved disagreeing with Andrea.

Janine pulled her key up from the bottom of her school bag.

"No one else is home."

"Right. Good."

Janine fed the cat while Sally looked around—she'd never been in this kitchen before, this tiny version of the big old house the Marsdens used to have. The thick nets and handmade rug were the same, though too large for the room. She thought maybe it was a new kitchen table, definitely new chairs—the old ones would never have fitted in. Janine made them instant coffee and Sally stopped herself just in time before she was rude about it. None of her group ever had instant coffee anymore if they could help it. Daniel said instant coffee was for plebs and if he couldn't have proper coffee he'd rather drink hot water with milk in it. He wouldn't have wanted that now though—not even to show off—it was UHT milk Janine was pouring into the mugs. But Sally smiled, took the mug, had a sip. Then they sat down at the kitchen table, Sally at one end, Janine on the corner beside her, the old ginger cat rubbing its muzzle on the soles of their school shoes, finally settling on the chair beside Janine. And Sally started on the rest of her script.

Being nice to Janine because that was what she was here for. Said how they all knew things had got out of hand, that she'd seen it sooner than the others, but that everyone knew now. Enough was enough. Apologized to Janine because that was what she was here for. Told Janine how much she liked her, really, honest, always had. Told Janine how it had all just started out as a joke, Janine knew that, didn't she? They hadn't meant to give her such a hard time, Sally in particular hadn't meant to give her such a hard time. She did remember they'd been friends before after all. Janine remembered that too, right? Sally was sitting close to Janine and then she stood up to make another coffee for each of them and when she came back to the table she sat closer still. She said it all, the words she'd rehearsed, and the whole scene played out just the way Will had said it would. Half of Sally's attention on what was going on in front of her, she and Janine at the kitchen table, half her mind amazed that it should be so easy, just as Daniel had predicted when Ewan dared to ask him what if it all went wrong: "Of course it won't go wrong, you twat. Janine Marsden's a moron.

123

Of course she'll believe it. Everyone gets off on it when people are nice to them—fuck, even Janine Marsden isn't that weird."

Will and Daniel had been sure it would all work out perfectly, even more sure than usual, and now Sally could see they were right. She watched Janine relaxing before her very eyes, saw Janine's flinching frown mask slide back into a calm face, a clear face. God, you know, maybe it was even a pretty face. With a proper haircut, and if she did something about those blackheads across her nose. She saw Janine's shaded dark eyes lift and look right into Sally's now, Janine properly turned towards her and looking her full in the face in a way she never usually did, hadn't done for years. And Sally thought perhaps this was all it took, maybe if Janine went into school tomorrow with her head up and the twitching frown missing, maybe if she just went in and smiled and looked straight ahead with her dark blue eyes, and surprisingly, really long eye-lashes, then maybe it would be different. Maybe it could stop. Perhaps all Janine needed to do was to stop acting like such a bloody victim and then the others might give her a chance. And even as she thought that, Sally knew it was too late. Too late for Janine to change and too late to stop now.

Sally was following instructions, Will's voice in her head:

"OK, so you reach over, and you take her hand—you guys, taking notes? Daniel? You bloody well need to. You're too clever by half, Daniel, and fuck knows, girls don't care about clever when they can have better. Trust me, this works every time … worked with Andrea anyway! Piss off, Andy, it bloody did too. Right, so you take her hand and you say some shit like, you know … I understand you or you understand me or we understand each other, some nice bollocks— but don't say too much, right? Your problem is, Sally, you always talk too much. Not this time. Leave it to her imagination. Let her think you're deep. Girls love it when boys say that crap. Yes, I know you're a girl, but it must be the same, right? I mean, Janine Marsden is a twat, but she is a girl. Anyway, you say some nice stuff, and then, you've got her hand in yours, OK? Your other arm goes over the back of her shoulder, nudge her in just a little bit closer, bend your head down. This is the good bit, you keep looking at her lips … not in her eyes, her lips. And there you go, she has to kiss you. Really. I promise. Oh, how much d'you want to bet, Ewan? I guarantee it. And you don't start talking about it, Sally. Just do it. If you start talking it all goes to shit. Don't give her a chance to ask questions or think about what she's doing. All right?"

All right. It was all right. Will's voice in her head, Andrea's snigger under her breath, Daniel's sneer swallowed back, Ewan's licked and leering lips kissed away, put away with this new feeling and these new kisses. Old kisses. Instead of her fears there were Janine's tight shoulders under her arm, relaxing, settling, Janine's calmer shoulders under her arm, bitten nail hand in her hand, dark blue eyes to her brown, now mouth to hers, lips to hers, and kissing her then. Real kissing now, not playing kissing. At the kitchen table, in Janine Marsden's house, with the big brother away in the army and her little brother at judo and her mum picking up the shopping and her dad working an extra shift and no one was getting tea ready. Not then. Not yet. Not now.

Sally was kissing Janine. Like she was supposed to, the way they'd planned that she would, like in the rehearsal Will made her and Ewan work on for the others. He'd wanted her to try it out on Andrea, but Andrea refused. None of that lezzie shit for her, not even for Sally to get the practice before Janine. Sally was so not going to snog Daniel, and no way was Andrea going to let her snog Will—Ewan would have to do. He didn't care and neither did Sally, that's what they said. And the rehearsal worked OK, and Sally and Ewan did the snogging and kept on doing it too, until Ewan went and tried to push his hand down the front of her top in front of everyone else and Will burst out laughing and she told them all to piss off. But it had worked then, more or less, and it was working now.

Sally was simply doing as she had promised, her turn to do the dare, face the task. Everyone else had a task when it was their birthday and now it was her go. Just turned sixteen and old enough to accept the group's challenge, whatever that might be. For Will it had been a shagging thing, Daniel's choice. Even though Andrea had already started going out with Will, she still agreed with the dare, it would be a way at getting back at a few girls she'd hated for ages anyway. And it wasn't really fucking around if she knew about it, so Will agreed. He shagged three different girls from their year in the same weekend, let each of them think he was cheating on Andrea just for her, told each girl he was going to drop Andrea Browne. And then laughed at all three of them together in front of the whole class on the Monday morning, loads of tears in the girls' loos at lunchtime, and a big fat smile on Andrea's face all afternoon. For Ewan it had been a break-in, into his father's own practice. That one was Sally's idea. Drugs and needles nicked, then Daniel's cousin sold them on somewhere else, and they all got pissed on the proceeds. For Andrea it was another sex thing; Will said it was only fair and Andrea couldn't disagree. Though afterwards she hadn't seemed quite as cheery about it as Will had. Afterwards she wondered if Will's dare had been that much of a hardship at all really.

Daniel's dare had been really hard to set up. It was all drink and drugs. Ewan's idea, typical. As many types of alcohol and as many different drugs as Daniel could down in an hour. It took the other four more than a week to get everything together, and even then no one managed to score anything harder than speed. No matter, Daniel had got really sick anyway. Sally thought the hash cake followed by Andy's famous Baileys-vodka-Cointreau cocktail was what had done it. Ewan blamed the speed-laced spliff. Whatever, Daniel hadn't even had a beer for almost a month afterwards. So they all took on their allotted assignment, and now it was Sally's turn. The youngest of the group, last to take a task, most eager to prove she wasn't a baby anymore. And Janine Marsden just happened to be the passing person the dare was played out on. Sure, she was someone who annoyed them all, who they liked to have a go at, she was a bit of an idiot. But it wasn't anything more than that. It never had been with Janine, she just annoyed them so they let her know it. Like any of the other dares, like those girls Will shagged, the guys Will picked for Andrea's blowjobs, like Daniel's poor liver, and breaking into Ewan's father's surgery, Janine Marsden was just some nobody, important only for the act of doing it. Nobody important at all.

Except that it was working. Sally knew it was working, she could feel Janine's surprise and then the yield and then, simply and easily, she felt pleasure. Sally could feel Janine's pleasure because it was what she felt herself. Exactly what she felt herself. And this was different to that French guy she'd got off with when they were away on that school trip. Different to getting off with that older bloke her sister was going out with too, when he came round and Cassie was out and he'd come on to her, and Sally only was thirteen, so she figured she might as well see what all the fuss was about. Which was nothing much as far as she could see; his mouth had tasted like stale cigarettes and his tongue was really big and slobbery and she'd thought it was crap, worse when his hands were bloody everywhere and her mum had come home just in time. Though probably that was just because she was young, only thirteen, maybe she would like it now. She liked this now. She liked snogging Ewan, the few times it had happened, and the little bit of touching they'd done. Not much, not enough to count, but some. Sally had always kind of fancied Will too, a bit at least, and she reckoned he sort of knew it, though of course Will Gallagher thought everyone fancied him anyway. Part of what she liked about fancying him secretly was that Will was Andrea's boyfriend, and sometimes she really wanted to give Andy a hard time, though she'd never dare do it to her face. Andy was way too tough to get into a scrap with. This one happening now felt different again though, like a whole new feeling. It was working on Janine. And it was working on Sally. And it wasn't playing.

She got up to go. Too quick, too hurried, knocked over a half-empty coffee mug. Half-full coffee spilled all over the table. The script wasn't quite done, Sally had not yet gone as far as they'd wanted her to, gone far further than she'd known she could. Sally was somewhere she didn't know she could go to.

"Don't go."

Looked at Janine Marsden and saw someone else. Saw herself kissing Janine Marsden and saw herself liking it.

"What?"

"Don't go yet. My mum won't be back for another hour, my brother doesn't get home from judo until late. You don't need to go."

"Yeah, I do. My … my mum will be wondering where I am … I've got go home. Sorry."

Janine's face went tight again, that flinch across her forehead. "Yeah. No. Of course."

Sally remembered her script, bad actress, faltering at the lines, not wanting to say them, too much truth in the playing, "Really, Janine, I do have to go. But maybe ... we could meet up again later? We usually go over to Will's place on a Thursday night, his dad's out then."

"All of you?"

"Yeah. Sooner rather than later? I do think we can make up, all of us. Make it better. I'll come and pick you up if you like? We can walk over together? You can come in with me. Seven-thirty?"

"OK then. If you'll come and get me," Janine smiled, face raised, dark blue eyes clear and bright, "if you like."

Sally picked up her school bag and ran out of the front door. Ran away from Janine. Ran back to the group.

TWENTY-EIGHT

The report was a press conference, an interview, a tribunal. Five of them gathered again in Ewan's parents' sitting room and a speeding slam of questions for Sally.

"So you kissed her?"

"Not at first."

"But you did."

"After a bit. Yes."

"Oh God! Gross."

Andrea thought it was vile. Even though she'd agreed and smiled and approved all along, she still thought it was gross. Would never have done it herself, so she said now. Though Sally wasn't quite sure how snogging Janine Marsden could be so much worse than giving blowjobs to five of the guys in their year, five guys they'd known since they were just little kids. But then Andrea's view of what was gross was slightly different from Sally's. Sally probably wouldn't want Will sitting there with his hand halfway up her shirt either. Probably. At least not while Daniel was paying such close attention.

"Yeah, but who kissed who?" Ewan wanted to know.

"Well, I did what Will said."

"Arm round her back, looking at her lips …"

"All of that, just like you told me. And then we kissed. I don't think it was me or her. We just kissed. Each other."

"And?"

"I really don't want to know."

"Shut the fuck up, Andy, we do."

The boys did want to know. Understood from their reading of cheap porn and Daniel's cousin's movie collection that they were supposed to care. Hot girl-on-girl action, the fastest way to a red-blooded boy's heart. Actually Will wasn't so interested in the kissing or any fumbling touch Sally was about to describe, he wanted to know where Janine was now, what she was thinking, feeling now. The lezzie part of it was irrelevant as far as he was concerned, it just made for better prospects in the long term, moved them on a little further to the next point.

Ewan didn't really care either. Well, he did, but only insofar as he would have wanted to kiss Sally himself. Wanted to be the one kissing Sally. Wanted to be the one snogging Sally, shagging Sally, fuck knows, maybe even loving Sally. Not that he'd say so here or now, but he had hopes. Daniel, however, did care about the girl sex thing. Someone had to. "OK, so real kissing, proper snogging, tongues and all?"

"Tongues and all."

"And then?"

And then Sally had felt something, something she didn't mean to feel, hadn't expected to feel—except maybe she had. Maybe she had known that was what she would feel and that was why she was so scared to do it and that was why she was so interested in the line of Andrea's breasts and the way Andy's Aunty Jane laughed with her head pushed right back and her neck so exposed and how Mrs. Stirling looked when she smiled in the kitchen and how she liked Will's Nana Tilly's army stories, all those women working together and no boys hassling them, goading them, and how his nan had said it was one of the best times of her life. The best time of her life. And maybe that was why, when Will first suggested the dare and Andy had said she was going to throw up at the thought and the other guys had just laughed so loud, maybe that was why Sally had said yes, OK, she'd do it.

Please. Maybe she wanted to do it. Back then, years ago, when it had been playing kissing and again now. Maybe she still did want to do it. And now she felt sick too. Sick the others would be able to see, sick she'd have to tell them, sick that maybe Janine knew and understood and had found her out. When Sally had only just found herself out. So much going on in her brain, mouth opening slowly, one word at a time, careful now not to implicate herself. Listening to the question and giving the right answer.

"Then nothing really."

"What?"

"Nothing really … much. Sorry, I freaked. It was too weird. I took off, went home for my tea and then came here. Like we agreed. Now we go to Will's place, right? Thursday night, it's what we do."

"Well, thank fuck for that."

Big sigh from Andrea, relieved that her only proper girl friend, the only girl she could bring herself to hang out with, and then mostly because it meant she got to be with all the guys without looking like a total slut, wasn't really such a fucking dyke after all. Andrea so scared of guilt by association. Sally guilty by association.

"No, hold on, Andy. That definitely wasn't the deal. You were supposed to do a bit more than that, Sally."

"Do something anyway."

"And snogging is not something."

Sally worried they'd send her back, make her try again, force her to feel it again. "Yeah, OK, well, it was a bit more than snogging."

All ears, all eyes, hands poised on jeans-knees. "What?"

Sally chose to tell them what they wanted to hear. Told them what she had imagined before now. Pictured and not even dared to tell herself she was thinking. Seeing herself fucking Ewan, who she certainly would, she'd thought about it often enough, though usually she imagined he was softer, smoother. Girlier. More girl.

"We … touched."

"Yes?"

"What?"

"Where?"

"How?"

The who was a given.

"Well, you know. I sort of … we just did stuff. I did, I mean. And then she did stuff back."

"Stuff?" A giggle and a snort, eyes rolled, lips licked.

"You started it?"

"You guys told me to. But Janine did more, way more. Like she knew what to do, I mean, of course I didn't know what to do. You

131

know that. That's the whole point of all this, right? But she did. She touched me."

"Where?"

"Here." Points. Lies. "And here." Indicates, physical untruth. "And … you know … there."

Will smiled, Andrea was disgusted, Daniel enjoyed the demonstration, wished it had been his idea, wished he'd thought of it before Will, wished he thought of anything before Will, except that he had kind of started it all that day in the playground, it was just Will had taken it further, always took it further. Ewan was unsure, waiting, worried about what next.

And then Will moved them on, giving orders. "Right then. And she's coming over later?"

"Yeah. She said she would."

"That's good enough for me. Phase Two, kids. Ewan, go get some juice."

"What?"

"Orange juice or something. Your parents have juice in the fridge, don't they?"

"Um, yeah … fresh. For the Vitamin C."

"Whatever. Get juice. Andy's got vodka and I …" rummage in his back pocket, sleight of hand and proud flourish "… have speed. Phase Two." Another burst of his favorite song, Andrea and Daniel exchanged irritated glances, and Will patted himself on the back at his own brilliance.

Later that night, fucking Ewan in his father's surgery, smell of alcohol wipes in the room and vodka-and-orange on their breath, acid stomach from the couple of speed balls they'd each taken, Sally opened her eyes wide against the picture behind her lids. She'd completed the task, achieved her dare, and so she got to have Ewan after all. Sally was sixteen now and her first fuck was well past its due date. Ewan was her coming-of-age gift from the group, her extra prize for completing the birthday task. Sally didn't want to think about Janine, not now, not again, and brought her mind back to the present. To what she was doing and where she was doing it and how she really did like Ewan. She thought about where she was and why she was and she also wondered if this was it. If, after all this time of pretty much liking Ewan, this was it. At sixteen Sally knew a great deal about how much she didn't know. And now, in the surgery, grinding away at each other, she had to ask herself if this was it. Even with the weirdness after what had happened earlier and knowing most people had a pretty routine first time—her sister had, even Andy said she had—she did wonder. If perhaps that hadn't been it, this afternoon, at the Formica table, that moment with Janine. Sally didn't know, but she kept her eyes open anyway.

Later that night, fucking Sally, Ewan delighted to be fucking Sally, delighted to be here and now and so glad to take his mind off everything else, all the other shit that had brought them here. This was where he wanted to be. But then again, right now he wasn't really thinking about Sally or Janine or any of the others. Nor did he know that Sally wasn't really with him. Ewan couldn't tell her thoughts were so far away; he was too scared and surprised and uncertain himself to notice her all that much. He hadn't said, of course, how could he tell that lot his truth? He'd told a story ages ago about some girl on their family's French holiday two years back, but this time was his first too. Terrifying, this first. And just odd really. Ewan hoped it was going to get better. Practice maybe, that might help. He wondered if Sally would want to try again. Later. Sooner.

Much later that night, Janine Marsden wondered to herself about how things worked out. How nice this afternoon had felt, how hopeful she'd been, waiting for Sally to come back and pick her up. Pleased and hopeful and then unsure, all over again so unsure. Janine covered her mouth with her hand, balled fist, tight fist, and held it all in and wondered if she really was what they said she was and if so, perhaps all she needed to fix it was to shag some bloke, every bloke. She wondered what made them think she was such a lezz, when all she'd ever done with another girl was kiss, just kiss, soft kiss, slow kiss. Janine wondered about it all, where it had started and who had started it and if it was all her fault as they said it was. She was hurting and sad and lonely and so tired of it all. Her mouth opened and closed again, and no words came out, she didn't know how to say them anyway and the day and night were running through her head and then it was too much and then she stopped thinking. It was easier that way.

TWENTY-NINE

Will was too famous to risk meeting with the others in public during the day, so they all went to Saz's for coffee instead. In Will's words, a quick meet and greet just to be sure they were coming from the same place. Saz didn't imagine that would ever be the case, but she couldn't be bothered explaining why not to him. And the sooner they met, the sooner it would all be over. She sent Molly off to work with assurances of a nice cozy day for stay-at-home mother and child, kisses at the door and random text messages of love. Then mother and child went out shopping for three people whose tastes, the taste of whom, Saz had known intimately at fifteen and sixteen and now she realized she didn't even know if they had milk in their tea, let alone skimmed or full fat. Though she thought it was fairly safe to assume all four could put up with organic semi if they had to. She bought coffee, milk, fat chocolate chip biscuits, and apricot cake. They lived in the grownup world now; surely no one was going to want marmite soldiers instead. Or cold fried egg sandwiches, Ewan's favorite. She picked up a couple of bottles of wine as well; if they didn't drink them at lunch she was fairly certain she'd need them by the time Molly came home in the evening. Then she grabbed a third. Just in case it turned really bad. Or good.

What happened was the same. Same and different, then and now. Four of five adults with their young selves slowly seeping out from under new haircuts and better makeup and considered clothes and aging skin and careful phrasing and knowing how to do it. How to meet people, to greet them, the tricks to play, words to say. Their youth selves shaped and molded and formed into the acceptable adult version, public face showing itself to the private past. It was a good act, an ordinary act, anyone could do it, everyone did. Saz looked around the room and saw how well the four of them had managed. Teenage rebels to adult variations on the success story.

Will with his televisual good looks and the CV all of them had watched, none of them needed to ask. Daniel's mask of cynical over-achiever turned nice teacher, helpful mentor, secret shagger. Andrea with photos of the husband and children first out of her bag; her honed body dressed in the regulation pastels her good wife image required. And Saz herself, classic example of the lesbian baby boom, forcing her triangular peg into a square hole and determined to make it work. All of it. Relationship, motherhood, work, family, friends, and this. This old-new thing that had forced its way into her life. Will greeted the others at the door like it was his flat. Andrea was comfortable with him, her wealth and his provided an easy meeting place. Daniel came into the room all arrogance and uncertainty—though Saz noted he eased a little when he saw Andrea. Saz was holding onto the photos for now; she didn't know when she'd use them, but figured it couldn't be that long coming. She showed off her daughter to the guests and then she opened the wine.

Four of five people stood in the room and looked at each other. Waited. Waited some more. The silence was solid until Will crashed through it. "A toast!"

"To what?" Saz asked.

Will smiled across the glass. "Us. Seeing each other again. Being here."

"Old times?" Daniel offered.

The two women exchanged glances, Andrea adding her own coda. "Better times, perhaps?"

Saz looked at her glass for a moment and then spoke up. "To Ewan?"

"OK." Andrea nodded. "Why not? To Ewan."

There was a lull which turned into a silence and then a yawning gap. The empty place where Ewan wasn't. Followed quickly by an awareness that Janine Marsden was waiting to hear from them.

Will spoke first. "Well, this is nice. The wine, the people. But, quite obviously, none of us really needed a reunion. Janine rang again yesterday. I told her we were seeing each other this afternoon. I said if she calls after two I'll let her know when we can meet."

"She's going to call here?"

"I didn't give her your number, Sally, calm down. She's going to call my mobile."

"You still don't have a phone number for her, any way for us to get hold of her?" Daniel asked.

Will turned to him. "No, I don't. Janine grew up too and she's clearly not quite as stupid as she used to be. I might not want to tell the authorities I've heard from her, she's counting on that, but she also knows well enough that I could afford to find her if I really wanted to. I thought it safest to play this part out on her terms anyway."

"So when do we see her?" Daniel asked.

"Well, for my own reasons, which I'm sure Sally has alerted you to, I'd like it as soon as we can. Though I don't imagine I'm the only one who doesn't fancy the idea of Janine Marsden dragging our collective pasts through their current life, right?" He looked round at the group, silent now, didn't bother waiting for an answer. "No. So. We'll agree a time with her and find out what she wants."

He looked around at the others. Saz and Daniel nodded, Andrea asked, "What did she say when you told her we were meeting?"

"Just that she was looking forward to seeing us."

Saz asked, "All of us?"

He nodded.

Daniel looked from Andrea to Will, "So where the hell does she think Ewan is?"

Will shrugged. "No idea, mate."

Will's mobile rang then and Saz watched as he composed himself before he answered. "Yes?" He listened for a while and then smiled and held out the phone to Saz.

"What?"

"Janine would like a word."

Saz shook her head, horrified, whispering, "No, I can't. Not now. I'm not ready."

Daniel grabbed the mobile from Will's hand and pushed it at Saz. "Take the bloody phone!"

Saz held the mobile to her ear. Opened her mouth to say hello but her tongue was dry. Janine heard her breathing.

"Sally? Is that you?"

"Mmm. Yeah."

"Hello."

She sounded the same. Not older but the same. Same Janine, and Saz could see herself the first day she walked away from Janine and into the waiting arms of what would become her safe little group. Same Janine, and Saz could see herself walking away from Janine's house that afternoon, ready to hand her over to the others. Same Janine, and Saz could see Ewan's body twisted and broken on the cold concrete.

"I'm really looking forward to seeing you, Sally."

Saz shook her head. Daniel was laughing at her, she couldn't do it, couldn't speak. She gave the phone back to Will, took Matilda from Andrea, Daniel wrote down the meeting time and place as Will agreed it. Tomorrow afternoon. Two p.m. After five minutes of haggling over venue, he finally gave Janine his own address. She wanted public as possible, he wanted the opposite. Janine let him win.

The others left soon after Will ended the phone call.

Saz closed the door behind her teenage years. She had less than a day to get used to the idea she was about to see Janine Marsden again. It had all happened so fast—even though she knew this was where they were heading, it had come too fast. But there was something else upsetting her, something she knew she wasn't quite getting. While they were waiting for Janine to call, Will had been laughing about Daniel's relationship with Becky. Saz carefully watched both Andrea and Daniel to see if any more evidence of their apparently recent relationship would emerge, but other than a sharper than usual remark about shagging underage girls, Andrea kept quiet. But she'd felt it then, something not right, other secrets not told. Saz knew it was stupid to rely on her feelings with this group, that of course they had all changed, they must have, but she also knew how very well she'd known them years ago. And despite the veneer of polite behavior this afternoon, she was sure there was something else she just hadn't quite grasped. Some other alliance yet to be revealed.

Saz shook herself into action. No matter how she was feeling, she had to get on, make this evening seem normal. If she didn't, she knew she'd want to tell all to Molly. And she couldn't imagine she'd ever want to do that. She sped through the flat, daughter-soothing, dinner-preparing, and running back over jump-cut flashes of their brief meeting. Daniel had said something when he'd just arrived in the flat and they were—the four of their five—finally all together again. Whispered something under his breath to Will about how while some people looked totally different, as if life had gouged itself into their faces, Andrea was just the same, if not more gorgeous. Saz had thought it dodgy given he was talking about Will's childhood sweetheart—and especially in light of what she now assumed she knew about Andrea and Daniel's recent or current relationship. But as she chopped the onions she wondered who he could have been talking about. In her opinion neither she nor Will looked all that different from how they'd been at school. Daniel's hair was thinner, Will had filled out, he was definitely man, no longer man-boy, but still very good looking, and despite one or two light wrinkles, she was probably slightly fitter than she had been back then. Apart from the beginnings of her gray hair and the wife-and-mummy costume she was wearing, this Andrea was almost identical to the sixteen-year-old version. None of them looked that different, not really. So maybe Daniel had been talking about someone else.

Then Molly turned her key in the lock and Matilda's face was a glorious smile and it was dinnertime. Here and now. New life, real life.

"What's going on?"

"How do you mean?"

Saz knew exactly what she meant. Her distractedness all that evening, the way she couldn't talk to Molly about anything to do with herself in case she told her everything, her eagerness to talk about Molly's patients in a way she never normally showed.

"I can hear your head, Saz. We've been together long enough for that. I know when you're here with me and when you're not. And right now, in fact for the past couple of weeks, you've been definitely not."

Saz could feel herself sinking, the desire to confess, to be heard, to be soothed. She trusted Molly to make it all better, always did. Only this time she didn't want to say it, didn't want to say anything. Her partner was looking at her, holding out her hand, offering warmth and understanding. Offering herself. Saz leaned in to kiss her.

"Piss off." Molly's body was eager, but her head was not that keen. "I asked what's wrong. And I may be cheap, but I'm not totally easy."

She was still smiling, still imagining that maybe it was something she could deal with, but Saz could see the small wrinkles at the corner of Molly's right eye—the right ones heavier than the left—could see the faint crinkling that went along with a slow-smoldering anger. She had to say something. So she chose the lesser confession over the bigger lie. Told the truth about the job for Claire. That she'd taken it anyway, asked Carrie to babysit for her, had done the work Claire wanted doing, sorted it all without Molly knowing, without disturbing Matilda, without a break in anyone's schedule. Without it mattering at all in fact. Except that in not telling Molly she had been holding back. And she was sorry. Really sorry.

"I'm glad you told me."

"You are?"

"Yeah. I knew something wasn't OK. In fact I thought at the time that I was probably wrong anyway."

"About what?"

"Not wanting you to work. I was feeling so bad about leaving Matilda myself that I just wanted to know you'd be with her. If both of us couldn't be here, then at least having one of us with her is better."

"No, Moll, really, I understand ..."

"I'm sorry, Saz. I should have listened to what you needed more. You've been brilliant about my dad, dealing with Matilda and all my grief and everything. I couldn't have asked for more support. I'm sorry, I should have trusted you to know if it was a job you could handle or not."

If Saz didn't know better she'd have sworn Molly was only saying all this to wind her up, to force the true confession from her. But she did know better. Did know that Molly trusted her, could see her partner was pissed off—but not with Saz, with herself for not being more generous. Saz couldn't have felt worse if she had told the truth.

"It doesn't matter. Honest, really. I shouldn't have done the job after we agreed I wouldn't. Or I should have told you. I hate not telling you things."

"I know."

Later that night, as she was falling asleep, Molly turned to Saz. "That was all, wasn't it? I haven't driven you away with all my crap?"

"Don't be stupid, babe. I love you. It's me who fucked up, not you."

"OK. Well, at least it shows we're a proper family now."

"How do you work that out?"

"That's what all good families are made of—half-lies and part-told secrets."

"Oh, and there I was thinking the model gay family would have to be better than the rest, that we might be the ones to finally get it right."

"Silly you."

"Silly me."

The next morning Molly's mother's neighbor called and saved Saz from having to find any further excuses. Molly's mother was sick. Not coping, not eating, not drawing the curtains at night, pulling them in the morning. Asmita had left her curtains closed for three days in a row now and when Shelagh went over to have a chat she didn't even ask her in. She'd opened the front door and looked out and past her neighbor, their conversation had been brief and stilted. Shelagh was worried, Molly was a doctor, as far as the neighbor was concerned, the solution was obvious.

Molly had called work and packed her bag within an hour. "Dad was always a doer, he got on with things, stopped her getting too low."

"You said this might happen."

"Ma's done pretty well until now. It's not that I don't think she should be unhappy, she should, she's lost her partner. But she's still here and I maybe need to help her move forwards."

"Fair enough. Poor Asmita."

"I won't go just yet if you don't want me to, I could wait until the weekend? Or you could come too?"

Saz didn't even need to think, opened her mouth and let it out. "I can't. I'm sorry. I promised Mum I'd help with Tony's party stuff."

"That's not until next week."

"Yes, and my brother-in-law's going to be forty and Cassie has decided it's this great big deal. They're really into the whole surprise thing. Two of the kids have nearly ruined the secret about a dozen times, and my mother is already in a severe state of panic that the combined efforts of me, you, my mum, Tony's mum, and her sister Mary can't possibly make enough vol-au-vents to feed sixty guests. I told her I'd go over and work through a plan with her and then start on some baking she can freeze. I'm sorry, I mean, I'll get out of it if you really want me to ..."

It was astonishing to Saz how easily she lied. Yes, it would be Tony's birthday and yes, she had offered to help, but it wasn't really that big a deal. And the detail that spilled from her mouth amazed her. Though she was stupid to mention baking. Saz really didn't like baking, Molly knew it. Surely she'd call her on it?

But Molly just smiled. And trusted her partner. "No, it's fine. It's easier if I go by myself anyway. Make a couple of extra cakes for me? I'd love to taste your efforts."

"Don't mock me. I'm being a nice sister-in-law." She was being a liar and a cheat. And getting away with it.

"OK, you take care of your half of the family, I'll take care of mine. I'll call when I get there and see what state Ma's in. I can't take more than a few days off anyway, so at the latest I'll be back Saturday afternoon, all right?"

"We'll have dinner waiting for you."

Saz booked the flight while Molly finished packing, then waved Matilda's hand as the cab took Molly off to the exorbitantly priced hour-long trip. Not for the first time Saz reflected on the fortune airlines must make from emergency flights. Then she called Carrie who, though she answered her phone as readily as she always did, was less keen than usual to come out and play.

"I just don't think I should."

"Things working out well with the new girl then?"

"They are, actually."

"Then bring her over with you. If it's a proper relationship she's going to be meeting Matilda sooner or later."

"Saz, you're not listening, I didn't say I wasn't free, I said I didn't think I ought to."

Saz's voice was calm but she found herself biting an irritated chunk out of Matilda's rusk, dry crumbs spiraling from her hand to the floor, the sweet biscuit rough on her tongue as she explained herself slowly.

"No, Carrie, I did hear you say it, but I figured that since ought and should were words you've been telling me to ignore for years, that you probably didn't mean to say them. Since when did you get so well behaved?"

"Look, it's not as if I don't enjoy being with your daughter and I certainly like having you pass me nice chunks of money every time I come over ..." Carrie took a deep breath. "But I just don't think you should keep lying to Molly."

Saz's laugh came out as a snort, rusk crumbs flying from her mouth. "Since when have you cared what Molly thinks?"

"OK, well not just her, but partly that. It's also because I feel like you're lying to me. Or not being totally honest anyway. You told me Ross Gallagher turned up out of nowhere, and I didn't even know you knew him. You're saying you need me over there, right now, but not explaining why."

"I don't have to tell you all my stories, Carrie, we're not lovers anymore."

"No, but I do know a lot about you, Saz, and it's weird that I don't know what's going on right now. I find it even weirder that Molly doesn't know what's going on either. I mean, if you were having an affair, I might understand …"

"It certainly bloody isn't that. I just need to go and see someone. It's a school reunion."

"With an urgent time imperative."

"Big word, Carrie."

"Don't try to put me off."

"I'm not, we're just trying to arrange a chance for some old school friends to get together. Will—Ross—has a busy schedule, he needs to meet today, and there's someone I need to talk to first."

"Right, and this is the same Will—Ross you greeted by telling to fuck off out of your home and screaming at me for letting him hold your baby?"

"I was surprised to see him, that's all."

"Bollocks. You're not telling Molly what's going on and you're not telling me what's going on, which makes me think something is going on that isn't good for you. And I may not be your over-protective partner, but I do reckon if you're not telling either of us what the problem is, then there's something you need to sort out …"

"Yes, there is. And I'm asking you to help me with it."

"No, you're asking me to help you hide it."

Saz was silent for a while, her anger at Carrie twisted around a core of fear that her old friend had found her out. She let the anger take over. It was far safer that way.

"Jesus, Carrie, you're a fucking hypocrite. You love it when I do things Moll doesn't know about. You always have."

"Yep."

"You get off on being my little helper and hiding things from her, it's like you get to keep a piece of me back for yourself."

"That's right, I do. It's something I enjoy about working with you. But I'm not working with you right now, I'm working for you, as a child-minder. And much as I can understand that in any long-term relationship there needs to be a few secrets, it's me that you're hiding from at the moment and I don't like it."

"So you won't help me? I can get you more money if you want."

"Piss off, Saz! Give me some credit, it's not about money. It's about you not telling me the truth."

Saz waited. "OK. I'm sorry. Fair enough. I will tell you about it. But right now there isn't time. I do need to go and see someone. And I do need your help. I'll tell you later."

"Promise?"

"Cross my heart."

"All right. I'll be there in half an hour."

"Where are you?"

"New girl's. She lives close."

With Carrie on her way, Saz sat Matilda down with a pile of colored bricks and pulled several cardboard boxes from the top of the wardrobe. In the third one she found what she was looking for, ripped a page from an old magazine, folded it into her bag. And then, having washed the old paper grime from her hands, she changed into proper, grownup, don't-fuck-with-me clothes. Stupidly expensive jeans she was usually too scared to wear in case they were ruined, a birthday present long-sleeved T-shirt where the lettering alone cost more than the bolt of fabric the piece was cut from, and a pair of green leather boots that never failed to bring a smile to her face and a kiss to Molly's lips. She was going to see Daniel's Becky again. The boots were her finest armor. Carrie was still slightly cool when she arrived. But she said the boots were fucking gorgeous.

THIRTY

The girl looked up as the door slammed shut. She was sitting alone. In the late morning light, with cigarette smoke soft-focusing her oval face, Saz thought she looked more than pretty, Becky looked like the fifties movie star she didn't yet know she could be. She hoped someone would get her a photo of Vivien Leigh or a young Elizabeth Taylor before too long, before the too-obvious French manicure and American-trash clothes became a habit and she lost all chance of the beauty she could still turn into. If only there was a role model for verging-on-the-edge-of-womanhood. If only the only role models weren't forty-year-old women pretending to be eighteen-year-old girls.

Saz asked for a coffee, waited while it was poured, then sat down in front of the child-woman and pushed forward the ripped piece of paper, a black and white photo of a school group. She pointed at one of the girls. "Do you recognize her? It's an old photo, but I need you to look carefully. Do you know her?"

Becky didn't deign to look down. "Hi, how are you? Lovely to see you again. How nice of you to agree to meet me at such short notice, really lucky you could make it."

"The woman, Becky. Do you know her?"

Becky raised her eyebrows, smiled, looked down at the photo, the smile fell into a frown. It was evidently not the face she'd expected to see, she opened her mouth to speak and then, thinking better of it, took a drag on her cigarette. She blew smoke directly into Saz's face—if not quite the looks, she certainly had the old-style star action—and traced her built-up fingernail around the curve of the face looking up at her.

"Why?"

"I want to know if you know her. If Daniel knows her."

"Do you know her?"

"We went to school with her."

"So he does too. Problem solved. Anything else?"

"I mean now. I want to know if he knows her now."

"Why don't you ask him?"

"Because I don't think he'll tell me the truth."

Becky paused, "And I will?"

"You might. If you were upset with him enough."

"Why would I be upset with him?"

"Oh, I don't know, because he was your teacher and he's been taking the piss. Because he was having an affair with someone else all this time. Because you were hoping for more from him than just the occasional shag?"

Becky didn't even flinch, put out her half-smoked cigarette and reached for another, flicking her enameled lighter with a practiced stroke. "How much?"

"So you do know her?"

"I might do. It's hard to tell."

"I know it's an old photo, and she's probably changed loads, but have a look. Do you know her?"

"How much?" Becky said.

"Fifty quid."

"Hundred."

"Sixty."

"No. One hundred. I mean it."

Saz looked at the girl and decided she did. She reached into her bag and pulled out a roll of cash. She counted off some notes, put the others away again.

Becky took the proffered cash, eyed the rest that went back in the bag, clearly pissed off she hadn't tried harder. "All right. The woman in the photo? She was at school with you lot?"

"This is a photo from then, yes."

Becky picked up the torn paper and stared at it, eyes squinting. She shook her head. "I don't know really. Honest I don't."

"A hundred quid for 'I don't know'?"

"She looks a little bit like this woman who used to hang around our college."

"You're sure?"

"No, I'm not sure. But I think … well, she looks a bit like her. I saw her a few times, most of us did. Only she wasn't around when we came back after the last holidays; they moved her out over the break, I think."

"What was she like?"

"Like a nutter, why else would you hang around the school gates?"

Saz didn't know, didn't want to. "Did she look sick?"

"No, not really. Just old. Like you."

"Thanks."

"You're welcome. Older than you actually. She looked older than you."

Becky didn't notice that her words had mattered. "Anything else?"

Saz waited, wondered if it was fair, if she was using Becky—maybe not as badly, but certainly with as little concern for the girl's feelings—just as Daniel had. And then, as she was starting to feel sorry for the girl, Becky swept another supercilious glance across Saz's face and down her body, taking in the clothes, the careful makeup, the gorgeous boots—the sharp heels a conscious attempt to add a mask of status—and grinned in slow comprehension. Becky still believed herself to be in charge. And if she believed it, she probably was. Saz realized that while she didn't especially want to hurt Becky, she wasn't all that worried about it either.

"Did you know Daniel was seeing another woman? Someone he cares about from a long time ago?"

It wasn't the question Becky was expecting, nor was it one she wanted to answer. But admitting her discomfort would have meant yielding power to Saz and Becky had no intention of doing that. "Yeah, actually, I did. How do you know?"

"Something she said when I met her the other day, the way she talked about him. Like she'd seen him way more recently than I had."

"That's it? Some female intuition crap?"

Saz smiled. "Yeah. And the fact that she's still using the same hiding place she used as a kid."

Becky wasn't fazed—or she wasn't showing it to Saz anyway. "So? It doesn't matter, Daniel can fuck who he likes. We both can. We agreed on that."

"And are you?"

"What?"

"Fucking other people?"

"None of your business."

"So you're not, but he is." Saz nodded. "Wow, you girls were so lucky to have all that girl-power shit, weren't you? It really made a difference."

"Yeah, right. And your burn-your-bra stuff was so fucking hot."

"I'm not that old."

Becky glared at her. "You are to me. Anyway, Daniel's got stuff he needs to sort out, about relationships and all."

"You really believe that?"

"She came a long time before me."

"Yeah. And they have history, a shared past. It's a stronger base for a shared future, don't you think?"

Becky did think and she didn't want to, she looked away to the counter, signaled for another cappuccino. "Dunno."

"Oh, come on, you're many things, Becky, some of them probably quite brilliant if you'd only give yourself a chance ..."

"Whatever. I can get plenty of patronizing at school, I don't need you doing it too."

Saz smiled, the girl was right, and it was all the permission she needed to be as hard as she wanted. "Fair enough. Truth is, I think you're useful to his ego, something for now, while he can't quite have the woman he really wants. That's what I think."

"You think a fuck of a lot. Why do you need me to agree with you?"

"Because I admit you probably know Daniel better than I do these days. I know he's been lying. I think part of what he's been lying about is this woman in the photo, and the other lie is about Andrea, the woman he's been having an affair with. He might like you well enough, playing with you probably makes him feel young

149

and clever, and I reckon he doesn't normally feel either of those very often."

"Daniel's work was really successful."

"That's right. Was. Once. He's not exactly a filmmaker now, is he? He might need you, Becky, to make him feel good, but it's Andrea he really wants. Don't you think?"

Becky stirred the froth into her coffee. "I don't know. None of this is news to me. He says he's been in love with this Andrea since you guys were at school. He told me all about her, it's not a secret."

"It is to her husband."

They smiled at each other then, the realization that perhaps Daniel and Andrea were well suited after all.

Becky poked at the old torn page from the school magazine. "What's it got to do with the bag lady? She's not Andrea, is she?"

"Definitely not. But I wondered if you'd ever seen her with Daniel, maybe he mentioned speaking to her? Or anything about her?"

"You don't want to ask him yourself?"

"No, I don't. Not yet."

Becky stared at her coffee, spoon circling, not answering. "Come on, Becky, another twenty quid and you tell me, yes? It's easy money. And I don't really think you owe him any favors."

Becky held out her hand and Saz passed over the twenty.

"All right. Yeah, it was quite sweet actually. They found her in one of the Portakabins. They were going to call the cops and get her moved out, but Daniel talked to her. Said he reckoned he could help her."

"When was this?"

"I don't know. A while ago, after the Easter break. He didn't do anything wrong. Everyone else didn't even care about her. Daniel was the only one who talked to her, he helped her."

"How?"

"Helped her find a place to stay, I think, talked to Social Services. You know how that lot always think teachers are so fucking sussed and responsible. It's weird."

Saz had to agree. "Yeah, it is."

"I don't get it. What's the problem with him helping her?"

"I'm guessing Daniel's been doing more than just helping her," Saz said.

"He's shagging her too? Oh, piss off!"

"No, I don't mean that. Just … there's been some stuff going on."

Becky scratched again at the edge of the photo and stood up. "Whatever. I don't care. Daniel and I are over now anyway."

"Did he tell you that?"

"No. I did. Pay for my coffee, yeah?"

Saz watched the girl walk out of the café, and wondered if Becky had any skills for heartbreak yet. And if it was ever possible not to blame the messenger. By the time the door closed behind her, Becky's phone was flipped open to text. But Saz wasn't worried she would call Daniel. Not yet, maybe never again. Like so many lovers before her, Becky had been able to cope with the existence of the other woman as long as she didn't have to admit to anyone else where Daniel's real affection lay. Now that it had been spoken aloud, made true in the telling, it was a very different matter. She got up to pay the bill. Apparently Becky's tab was for fifteen coffees, six croissants, and eight full breakfasts.

THIRTY-ONE

Janine walked towards them, head held high, shoulders back, arms loose at her sides. Walked carefully, confidently, like she was fine about walking, about being there. She'd got out of bed early this morning. Dressed especially for today, made herself look right, look like them. Like she belonged.

Janine Marsden was scared. But then she was always scared. This wasn't any different to every day every time every walk to school. She was a scared person, always had been, always would be according to her mum, unless she did something about it, took a stand, but even then, maybe she shouldn't push it. Her mum didn't like to push anything. But Janine had made up her mind, and today would be different. She'd thought about it all night, twisting her aching body in the hot sheets, rubbing her crying eyes until the tears-red was impossible to differentiate from the rubbed raw. And she'd wondered if it might be possible to change. Now, after this had happened. She tried to talk to her brother about it, before breakfast, as he stood at the bathroom door, but that was no good, all he ever said was you'll only make things worse, it will be better when we grow up, adults are nicer, they try harder. For now just stay out of their way, they only want you to pay attention to them. Ignore them and they'll go away. But she couldn't ignore them anymore and they hadn't gone away and now here she was, walking up the street towards the school gates, fists screwed up, serrated fingernails grazing her sweaty palms.

Weeks and months of bringing herself to this moment, hoping to make a difference, force a change, and then yesterday afternoon, actually talking to Sally after all these years, friends again maybe, more now maybe, and finally it had seemed possible. But then there was last night. Well, anyway. That was done, the night had passed. Everything passes. And Janine promised herself she was going to sort it out. Work out why they were like this. She would ask them. Not just take it, not just behave as if she deserved it, but actually ask them. Ask the question she should have asked ages ago. She was going to talk like them. She had made a real effort to look like them, be like them. Janine had it figured, if she was like them—talking, walking, looking—then they would have to tell her, explain themselves. They'd have to answer the question: Why are you doing this to me?

One by one. Asking each one. The boy-man Will Gallagher, the one every girl in the school fancied. So did she, Janine did too, she admitted she was the same as them, same as all of them. Or maybe not. Maybe that kiss, those kisses with Sally, did mean something else. Mean what they'd been accusing her of all along. Then there was the other guy, Daniel, the tall thin one, the clever one, too clever. The youngest guy, Ewan or Evan or whatever his name was, Christ, she wasn't even sure she knew his name, but God knows they all knew hers. And the two girls. Andrea Browne. So totally hard, maybe she'd never get through there, but yes, OK, maybe even Andrea was worth trying, appealing to, getting an answer from. Janine was prepared to give them all a chance. More than they'd ever given her. And Sally. How nice she'd been yesterday afternoon, how nice it was yesterday afternoon. Not twenty-four hours ago. The hopes and the maybe and the touch. Too much touch, not that touch, no more touch. No more.

Sally goes on ahead, tells Janine she's going to check it's all OK, tells the others it's now. Janine's here, walking up the street. Janine rings the doorbell to Will Gallagher's flat over the sweetshop. Sally comes running back down to answer it. Tells her it's fine, come in, come on in. Everyone wants to see her. Janine follows her up the stairs and behind her back Sally reaches out a hand, a welcoming hand. Janine takes it, holds Sally's soft hand and knows it will all be OK now. She's holding Sally's hand. They walk in the room together and Will Gallagher comes over first. He's holding out a glass. Vodka and orange he says. Welcome he says. We're so glad you could come.

Perhaps she'd got it wrong. How Sally had been in the afternoon, how they'd all been in the evening. Perhaps she just didn't understand. She didn't understand, would never understand, she wanted them to explain, to help her make sense of it. She'd left home happy enough, hopeful enough. Her mum was dozing in front of the telly and her dad wasn't home from his extra shift yet and her little brother was upstairs listening to music or writing his crap lyrics or wanking. Or all three. Sometimes it seemed to Janine her little brother could probably do all three at once. Sally had promised she'd go and talk to the others, try and fix things, maybe she had. Maybe that was what Sally meant by fixing it. Maybe it was normal for them. Usual. It wasn't normal for Janine. Janine didn't understand normal any more.

They finish the first vodkas really fast. Andrea makes more, less orange juice this time. And then another round. A line of speed. Janine hasn't taken drugs before. Didn't know that they did, not for definite. She's heard the rumors of course, but—like most of the kids in their year—she assumed it was a rumor Daniel Carver had started about himself. Lots of kids talk about dope, get stoned at weekends, but this is different. This is officially hard drugs. Don't feel hard, feel fast. Better than vodka, better than the leaflets said, the ones they'd been given in third year. Just Say No. Janine says yes. They are being nice to her. Andrea talking to her. Andrea Browne listening to her. Janine isn't used to drinking, unaccustomed to drugs. She doesn't have a group to practice with like this lot. But Sally is still smiling and Daniel has changed the music to something he's had sent over from America, some movie soundtrack his cousin wanted him to hear. Rare, he says it is. Imported. Janine thinks it sounds harsh and weird, long lines of shouted lyrics she can't make out and screeching guitar that sounds tuneless to her, a woman's voice that is more off-key than on. But she doesn't

*say so. Just nods, looks interested. Tries to look interested. She
checks her watch, it's getting late, an hour has passed without her
even noticing, the music is louder, Will whispering to Daniel.
Janine is worried about her dad, scared he'll get home before she
does. Worried she'll get into trouble, but Sally says don't worry,
what's getting in trouble with your dad, when everything else is
going OK? Whispers, what do your mum and dad matter when
these guys are being nice to you? They're being nice to you. And
Sally's right. It's all going OK. Until it isn't.*

She'd been thinking about it all night. No sleep, no sleep at all.
Wondering how it happened and what she'd done to let it happen
and why they would have done that anyway. Janine didn't even
think it was that weird when Will came over to where she was sitting on the sofa with Sally and started kissing her. Later she figured
perhaps the vodka and the speed had played a part, but at the time
it seemed to make sense. After all, Sally had kissed her. Shit, maybe
it was what they all did. Maybe that was why they liked each other
so much, maybe they just all fancied each other, did it with each
other. Janine knew it was weird, wasn't as if this sort of stuff happened on primetime TV. Not much anyway. But it was happening,
then, to her, and she didn't know any better. That's what she'd
have told her mum, if her mum had listened, if her mum had been
awake when she came back in last night. If her mum had had time
to talk this morning before going to work.

*Janine knows it's weird, but at the time, in the half light at Will's
place, it seems like a good idea to go along with them. A way to
make it stop, make them stop being mean. And anyway, Janine
knows they think she's strange. Maybe they think she's like them.
Would like them. After all, he is Will Gallagher, everyone—every
one of the girls—wants to kiss Will Gallagher, right? And she
thinks she certainly wouldn't mind pissing off that bloody Andrea
Browne, sitting there glaring at her from the armchair, watching
her boyfriend Will sit between her and Sally and lean into her and*

kiss her. Janine's eyes open past his cheekbones and see Andrea glaring at her there. So she kisses him back, figures that might be good enough. It had been for Sally. The kiss, the slow touch, the smile. But then quickly, too quickly, it isn't enough, just to kiss Will Gallagher, nowhere near. And when she gets home Janine understands even less than before.

So now she was going to ask. Just get it all out in the open. Ask them what the fuck was going on. Ask them, why her? What had she ever done to make them pick on her? She would take them in turn, one after the other, and ask her question. She would walk to their place, find them before they found her. She was going to walk up those steps by herself and right up to them in their hidden-away corner of the grounds. They would have to answer her then. It was a civil, sensible question. Quietly, politely, and they would be surprised. She would speak to each one—it would be weird if they didn't answer, they would look silly, and Janine had read the problem pages, devoured the answers the sensible agony aunts gave, she knew that above all they would hate to look silly. Will Gallagher hated looking silly. She would get in first, confront them with the facts, lay it out. This has happened.

Will kisses her and his hand moves across her body, down her front, from her breasts to her stomach to her thighs, she starts to pull away but Will's arm is tighter than it was before and then Andrea is leaning over them both, she's not in her armchair now, there's a pair of scissors in Andrea's hand and she's telling Janine to take off her shirt, take it off or I'll fucking cut it off.
    And this.

Janine half naked and Will's hand on her skin, her body. Her body. Ewan laughing with Sally in the corner, snogging with Sally in the corner, and Andrea's big art room scissors chopping at Janine's good shirt, little bits of material falling off on to the old carpet.

Daniel has a camera. Daniel Carver has a camera, and he's taking photos, Will is turning Janine to face the camera and he's telling her to smile and they're all shouting it out now: Cheese! Say cheese! Say cheese, Janine! Please say cheese, Janine! Say cheese please! And Daniel is all excited because these are such good photos, his new camera. He's been saving for ages and his cousin's mate has a darkroom and he'll print the photos up. All of them. Then Janine Marsden can see herself. See what they all see. Show her mum and dad and the other kids at school what they all see.

And this.

All three of the boys standing around her, tight around her, pushing in on her and Daniel still taking photos, leaning in, taller than the others, the flash shining too bright in her eyes, and the girls, Sally and Andrea, drinking from the vodka bottle now, last few drops, sharing the last few drops and the music is so loud, the music Daniel thinks is so cool is so loud, so strange. Now Janine is on her knees between the three boys, three men. They look like men from where she is, from down here, from nowhere else to go and she's asking the girls to help her, pushed down because Daniel said she looked better that way, better from there, it would be a better picture, better angle, and Andrea and Sally are laughing, holding each other and laughing and Daniel is saying this is a brilliant shot, great shot, yes yes baby, do it baby, one more time, come on baby, oh yeah, oh yeah, you've got it, that's it, that's it. And they're all laughing. Laughing at her. Sally is laughing at her. And Janine knows this was Sally's idea too. That this has been Sally's idea all along. Janine knows this afternoon was all a part of the same long night. And knowing that she doesn't feel so drunk anymore. She finds the strength to push them aside—not really so hard, they're laughing so much, easy to push away now—and gets to her feet, finds a shoe, drags her skirt down round her knees. Her shirt is on the floor, arms cut off, big hole cut out of the back. Her good shirt, Janine only has one good shirt. And she'd worn it for them because Sally had asked her over and it was all going to be all right. Janine wants to be sick, wants to throw up, wants to lie down and pretend

*this is not happening, has not happened, but most of all she wants
the film out of that camera, has to get the film and scrabbles over
the others, Ewan and Will laughing so much they've collapsed on
the settee now, or maybe that's the speed too, making them laugh,
laugh so much, laugh at her. So Janine grabs the camera out of
Daniel Carver's hands and he's shouting at her telling her to be
fucking careful, that cost a lot of fucking money you stupid bitch,
but she has the back off it now and there's no film. No film inside
the camera. And now it's really fucking funny, all that fear and
shame and horror and there's no evidence, no evidence at all.
Nothing to send to her mum and dad, nothing to put in the school
magazine, to make leaflets that go under the windscreen wipers on
the teachers' cars. None of their threats to come true. Just the five
of them laughing, collapsed and exhausted and laughing.*

Then this.

*It changes again. Janine is not ready and she is not willing, but she
doesn't know where to go, how to leave. And part of her thinks
perhaps this will be an end to it, this one last thing and then it will
be over and they'll leave her alone. And part of her thinks this is
what Sally must have meant all along, to get her back here to Will's
flat and for this to happen. And part of her does not think at all.
Then much of her does not think at all. There are knickers
wrenched away, a tight elastic line that will leave a banded bruise
the next day. There is some kissing too. But it isn't soft and it isn't
nice and it doesn't make you feel good in the pit of your stomach,
behind your knees, your lower back. She thinks that maybe Will
Gallagher is kissing her because it's what you do—this thing, then
the next—but Janine Marsden has no experience and it hurts. It
hurts when he pushes his mouth against hers and it hurts when he
pulls her legs apart and it hurts when he shoves his penis inside her
and it hurts when he rocks himself back and forwards in her body.
Out of her body. Janine Marsden is a long way out of her body. And
staying away. So even though Daniel Carver stands over her next,
she doesn't really see him, feel him, what he does. And anyway, it's
all so fast, all happens so fast, and then Andrea Browne is telling*

the guys enough, she's bored now, enough, and Sally is just sitting there, leaning against Ewan, her eyes closed, muttering about how pissed she feels, like she's not really there, like it isn't all her fault. And Janine pulls on what's left of her bra and her good shirt and shoves her laddered-tights feet into her shoes and grabs her bag and runs down the stairs, out of the flat, door banging behind her, runs all the way home. All the way home. And hides in her room in her bed and doesn't answer when her dad gets in even later than her and calls goodnight. Doesn't have any answer to give. Not quite ten at night and fast asleep already. Her dad hopes she's done enough homework.

So after that, after all that, wasn't it time to stop now? Janine would make them see the sense in what she was saying. They must see it had gone too far. Now. Janine wasn't going to tell anyone, not even her mum. She wouldn't make a fuss, they didn't need to worry about her making a fuss. It just needed to stop, she'd had enough. It only made everyone feel uncomfortable, her of course, but maybe too the five of them, definitely all the others standing round, the next circle out and the next. All the others in the No Ball Games playground who felt it too, who froze up just as she did when their little group came into view. And they must feel odd now, after last night. They had to.

Why are you doing this to me?

Obviously she had said something wrong once, something she'd done, failed to do, and now they didn't like her. Maybe she had upset one of them. Andrea perhaps. Maybe they'd picked up her thoughts about them, how she secretly thought of Andrea as slutty. And nowhere near as good-looking as she thought herself. There had to have been a first thing, first time. The first time she said a wrong word or wore the wrong clothes or took someone's chair or ate too much or smiled too little or hell, you know … something.

159

It must have started sometime, though Janine herself couldn't remember when, just that it had been like this for so long and didn't seem to be getting any better, no matter what she did. And then they'd made it even worse. Sally had made it even worse. Janine could not make herself invisible. She had tried for so long and she had failed. She knew that now. No matter where she hid, they always found her. But she would be happy to put things right. If only they would explain themselves, then perhaps it could all be sorted out. And she'd start with the obvious.

Why are you doing this to me?

They were startled at first. Had seen her coming, watching from the vantage point where they could see and yet not be seen. Not unless they wanted to be. They were talking to one another, what they would do in the weekend, whose homework they should copy. They were not talking about what had happened last night. Daniel and Will looking at each other, keeping it between themselves. Andrea holding some secret, wittering on about the celebrity scandal in the paper instead. Sally keeping her thoughts to herself, not sure how to be with Ewan, Ewan practically ignoring her because he had no idea whether she wanted him to talk or not. No one really wanting to know. Then Sally, sitting on the edge of the wall, saw Janine Marsden walk round the corner into the concreted yard and, not sure what she was seeing, worried about how long they would wait before it started. It always started. Sally thinking today wasn't a good day, it didn't feel right this morning, not after that, last night. And Janine looked strange too, walking directly towards them, heading up the steps. Andrea noticed it as well, but her reaction was different, the guys weren't really paying her enough attention, embarrassed maybe, after what had happened, fearful they'd gone too far, but she wanted their attention. Wanted it back from Janine.

Ewan felt as stupid as this idiot coming towards them, her mouth open and words falling out, muttering some shit, mouthing some shit. He felt weird about last night at Will's place and weirder still about him and Sally in his dad's surgery. He wanted to talk to Sally about it and didn't know where to start, what to say, wanted to tell everyone and wanted to keep it entirely private. He had no idea what to say to Sally, though he did want to talk to her, quiet and easy, because he did like her, really liked her. And at the same time he wanted to tell the whole bloody school he'd just fucked Sally Martin. Both and neither. All and nothing. And now here was Janine Marsden looking even madder than when she'd run off last night. Well, at least this was better than worrying about how to talk to Sally.

She was speaking. Or shouting. Janine Marsden was shouting. Daniel turned in surprise. This had never happened before. Will leaned back and smiled. He was amazed. And delighted. Janine Marsden was talking to them, at them, walking towards them, right across the no-play-ground and up the steps, shouting now, louder and weirder. Off her fucking head she was. Incredible. You know, either she was very brave or totally insane. Either way, it looked like fun.

Until it didn't.

THIRTY-TWO

"Why are you doing this to me?"

It was easy enough to say. Janine was stunned it came out of her mouth so fast. Flowed and circled and twisted and turned and the words ran right round their legs, crossed their arms, up and over their heads, the science block, the maths room, over one side of the steep roof and back down through dirty gutters, dirty school gutters full of hidden cigarette butts and into toilet blocks where crying girls threw up a family-forced breakfast and small boys wondered when were they ever going to grow up ever going to get it right ever know what to say when to say how to say.

Janine Marsden opened her mouth and out it came. Clear and confident, exactly as the agony aunts had said. Just you go up to them. Ask them. You might as well, they're going to pick on you anyway. What have you got to lose? Confront them. Bullies can't stand confrontation, they hate it, it's why they're bullies, so they have the power, so they're in control. Trip them up, play them at their own game, just ask it. I dare you. Just ask it. Go on. Ask. What are you afraid of? How much worse can it be? I dare you. Daring herself.

"Why are you doing this to me?"

Now she was close, now they could see her properly, they were horrified. It was ghastly. Not even funny. And it was embarrassing. Janine Marsden standing there, mouth open so wide her lips had cracked at the edges. Moving her mouth, beating her little balled bitten fists. Like she was speaking, like she was shouting at them, shouting it all out. If it carried on much longer the teachers would know who she was shouting at, the whole fucking school would know who she was shouting at, standing there in front of the five of them, shaking and mouthing off. Someone had to shut her up, someone had to make it stop. Will took a step forward. Her mouth opening and closing and all those words about to come flying out. Only there was no sound, no words. Her eyes wild and those weird fucking clothes she was wearing. Was her jumper on back to front? Her hair piled up on her head, all over the place, so messy. Some really bad eyeliner work going on there. Nothing like she usually looked, none of the hidden mouse like she usually looked. It was gross really. And she was just there with the five of them. No one coming to get rid of her, take her away, fix it, not yet. No one to see what was going on. No one in charge. Yet. Will took charge.

He moved forward then, fast, moved forward to grab Janine's hand. The one she was slapping her face with, standing on the edge of that little wall, standing there and about to bloody well go over if she wasn't careful, beating herself up like some mad woman, she really was a mad woman. Will pulled her in close, wanted to grab her hand before she really hurt herself. And then, and he was only trying to fucking help, then she really went off on one. Totally crazy. All he was doing was trying to help, get her away from the edge of the wall, and she was spinning in his arms, she started screaming and fighting out like he was going to hurt her or hit her or rape her or something, as if, as if he'd want to screw her, right? Janine Marsden? I mean, as if. He pointed that out right there and then, to anyone who'd listen, to all of them listening, as if he'd want to touch her. Janine fucking Marsden? You've got to be kidding. Daniel Carver backed him up, Andrea Browne laughed out loud at the idea. Laughed out loud at something anyway. Insane she was, had to be, totally mad bitch. But Janine's screaming had no sound and though the hands tried to reach Will, it was herself she was beating off, beating up. Then Ewan tried to help, thought he had an idea. Some crap about his dad being a doctor, his mum being a nurse, you know how kids always think they can do what their parents do, think they pick it up by osmosis, and Ewan had always wanted to be a doctor and he'd been in the surgery often enough, it was part of his own house, for God's sake, and he had this idea he could calm her

163

down, get in there, slip between Will and Janine Marsden and the fists with which she was beating herself up. Only he didn't.

Janine was elated, so pleased with herself. She'd said it now and told the truth, asked them why and dealt with the questions and faced her fears, spoken it all, right out loud. Her own voice flying over the school buildings, out into the street, past all the people walking to work and on the top floor of the dirty buses and up to where the laughing magpies sat watching from the tops of the trees. Janine had said all the words she knew, all the words to make them answer. She wanted Sally to know how it felt, what she'd done, so she said the words, to make them understand. And Janine could see that he was trying to make it better, the boy beside Sally, the one nearest to her now, Ewan. Sally didn't seem to understand, but maybe that boy did, maybe the agony aunt was right, all she had to do was ask. She wanted to ask Sally why, she needed to get close in, close as she could, to ask Sally why she'd done this, to get her to understand what had happened, what she'd done. Sally looked on and really didn't want to see. Didn't want to understand.

But then Ewan got in between Janine and that little concrete wall, somehow he pushed Will out of the way and wedged himself between Sally and Janine. And then Janine's eyes were closed, and she was hitting, at herself, out at herself. And Sally was terrified, hating it, scared of it, the action and the no-sound and the awful, horrible pictures of what had made this happen and she didn't want to see, didn't want to know. Sally put out her arms, pushed Janine away, needed her to get away, she was too close, it was all too close. Will still had hold of Janine's hand, hurting her. Janine pulled away from him, from Ewan, reached for Sally, twisted herself, and then Ewan wasn't helping anymore, and he wasn't in the way anymore, and there was a clear route straight to Sally that Janine was going to take, would take. But Ewan was falling. All the way down. Right down.

And when Ewan reached the ground he wasn't OK like Will Gallagher had been that time he'd jumped down the wall. And he didn't just sprain his ankle like Daniel Carver had when he'd tried to do it too. And the sound of Ewan's landing made Andrea throw up, vomit rush to the back of her throat and out onto the concrete steps. The sound of slam and then crunch and then snap. One after the other. Slow motion noise. Slow motion Ewan. The snap was the loudest. Ringing on long after he'd stopped.

And Sally never got to ask Ewan what he thought about that first ever sex, loss of virginity, such a big deal moment in every young person's life. Hers. Theirs. His. Maybe his. She thought maybe it had been his.

THIRTY-THREE

Sally walked down the steps. There were twenty-three of them. One foot after the other, one movement—hip/knee/foot—after another. Right, left and right again. Walked as if it was what she always did. She always did. She never had before. Never had walked down these steps in silence before, not that she could think of, not that she could think of anything, but it was so quiet, this place was never quiet. There was always noise, talking, other kids shouting, jeering, laughing, shouts bouncing off brick walls, people leaning out of windows, Will behind her, Daniel in front maybe, Sally and Andrea jostling between them, movement and action. Stopped action, she remembered something from a science class, stupid thought, irrelevant there and yet it felt important, she let it stay. Kinetic and latent energy. Sally's was all latent energy, waiting, and yet she was moving. Downwards. Down the steps.

Janine said: "I didn't. She said. Sally said. They wanted to. Like me. Friends. She was with me. We were. And I don't know why. Why? Why did they? Last night. That. Why did they? It was so nice. Afternoon. Yesterday. My friend. It was nice. We were. How does that happen? How does it happen when they change? I don't. I don't understand."

And then Janine waited.

And then Janine said: "I heard him falling. Like wind. Like holding your hand out against the wind."

No one heard Janine's words. Her mouth moving against the wind.

Ewan lying at the bottom of the concrete block wall. Ewan stopped like he'd never started.

Teachers running from all directions and no time at all before the siren started. Sirens. All that noise. The ambulance rolled right up, through the gates, driving across the white lines for knee-grazing netball, right up beside Ewan. Not Ewan. Stopped Ewan.

Hard to get down the steps, down to him. Hard to get past the push of other kids. A ring of them. Not that they were that close. Not as close as when there was a fight. They were arcing round him, the other kids, a body's length away. Ewan's body the radius of their semi-circle.

And after they'd told the Headmaster what had just happened: he fell, she went crazy, he fell, they told it all over again to the nice policewoman, and the serious policeman. And then another nice policewoman started again, new questions. About why.

Will said: "I've got no idea, none at all. She just came in the gates and launched into one. It was totally fucking weird—I'm sorry, I mean, it was weird." Smiling at the policewoman, not the kind of boy to use bad language, not in that company anyway. Nice manners. A good smile, something more than good, more to offer. Continuing, "It was just, you know, weird. We were up on the top there, it's where we go, we always do. My girlfriend and me, a few mates of ours. Everyone knows it's where we go. Us. We sort of hang out there. We do have permission to. And you can see down to the gate. She looked really weird from the minute she came into the playground, I had no idea what she was on about. Still don't, sorry. Yes, like I said, we were all together last night. After school at Ewan's and then my place. My dad was at work. It's what we do on Thursday nights. Janine popped in. She didn't stay long."

They had thought about this, agreed on this, had this discussion first thing this morning. All five had spent the evening at Will's place. Janine had popped over, some talk about school, then she left. No big deal. And then they had all gone home, their separate ways. Just like normal. Sally and Ewan had been shy about people knowing what came later, didn't even tell the others what came later. Sally had been going to tell Andrea, later. Better for them all to say they were together, Sally wasn't ready to say they'd been alone, just her and Ewan. The others figured what had happened, of course, but none of them had taken the piss, not yet, not even Daniel. Sally was grateful to them for that. Had been grateful, until Janine arrived.

Will was finishing up with the policewoman, regretful smile: "I'm sorry I can't help more. Really. I guess she's just not OK."

Andrea said: "No ... I don't know. We were together last night. Will and I. Sally and ..." She wiped her running nose, fat tears pooling illicit mascara under her eyes, mouth bitter with bile. "... and Ewan. And Daniel." Telling the story. As arranged. "We were all together. At Will's. We're always all together, Thursday nights, everyone knows that. She came over, didn't stay long. That's all. I don't know what she's ... what she's ... I don't know. I'm sorry. I can't do this. I want my mum." Andrea ran off, into the girls' loo, three would-be friends, could-be gossips following her in.

Daniel said: "He's our mate. Ewan's our mate. She's a mad fucking bitch. She just went off on one. What are you talking to us for? We spent the evening at Will's." Most of it true, most of the truth. "Why are you asking about us? We didn't do anything. She just went off. Everyone saw her. Fucking idiot."

Daniel kicked at his chair, holding his hands tight, fists in folded arms. Angry at himself and angry at Janine Marsden and very very angry at Ewan for getting in the way. For falling. For stopping.

The nice policewoman was trying to work it out. Horrible accident, horrible school stuff, kids at school. The policewoman was young herself, it wasn't long since she'd been at school. Hated school, never fitted in, never managed to find herself a group like this little lot. She could imagine what they were like. Looked down at her skirt, smoothed it over her knees. She loved her new uniform. The new blue uniform that held her safe.

Sally said: "I'm sorry, I don't know either. I just went out with my mates. With us. We always go out with us. You know, just hanging round, whoever's place is free. It's what we do after school, weekends, evenings if we don't have too much homework or it's not exams. My mum always wants me to stay in to revise when it's exams. Well, sometimes we go to ... to Ewan's place. Saturday mornings always. Yesterday afternoon we just hung out. Thursday nights we go to Will's. Nothing really. I mean, some of us smoke, sometimes, but that's not a big deal is it? Only cigarettes I mean. We were all together. At Will's. It's what we do." Sally with Ewan and holding Ewan and kissing Ewan and he holding her and kissing

168

her and both of them wondering if this is it and if they're OK and if they're doing it right. If it's right after what has happened, if it's right that they should be here at all, if this will help them forget what else there was. "I went home for tea and then in the evening we were just all at Will's. His dad was at work. Nothing really, talking, whatever. It's what we do when we're together. Nothing really."

And then Sally said quite clearly, specifically, "I don't know why she was upset. I don't know what she's talking about."

Kids were sent home from school and the piece of ground where Ewan had fallen was cordoned off. Blue and white police tape, just like on the telly. Ewan picked up and put in a black zippered bag and into the ambulance just like on the telly. Sally went to find Andrea, get her back from the clutches of other girls, eager for the danger and drama to rub off on them. Andrea and Sally in a shared cubicle, like when they took speed together at parties, only crying now, not giggling. Will and Daniel talking quietly, waiting for the girls, their girls, suddenly men taking care of the little ladies, arms around the girls. Taller arms around the small thin girls. Form teacher guiding them into the sick bay and their parents coming for them, phone calls made, work left, on their way.

Shock and a cup of hot sweet tea. Everything too real to feel it. Too slow, too fast. Four not five. Nothing like on the telly. The driver didn't bother with the siren as the ambulance drove out.

THIRTY-FOUR

They wore black. Ewan's parents had asked people to wear bright colors, spring colors, his favorite season they said, but the four of them wore black. They did it because Will said it was only right, they were his best friends. They did it to stand out and to stick together. They did it because Ewan's mum was wrong. Spring was back to school and compulsory PE and heading for summer, which Ewan, pale-skinned and more bored with every year, had enjoyed even less. Those fancy family holidays where his parents fought most evenings and pretended to be happy most days, the too-hot beaches and the warm south European water. Ewan had thought Blackpool sounded great, Scarborough might be good. But he'd never been to either, his parents insisted on abroad. Ewan had really liked winter, just as he liked rain and dark, serious, moody boy-music. He liked black and dark gray and polo neck jerseys and long-sleeved shirts and thick dark socks. His favorite outfit was his dead grandfather's black suit. He'd been hoping to grow into it. And his mother was his mother, and she was really upset, and the Stirlings had every right to ask whatever the fuck they wanted— Will was very clear about that as well—but she was wrong about spring, they were wearing black. Besides that, it was spring now. Not so good then, was it? In the end Mrs. Stirling wore black too. When she tried to put on the pale blue skirt and jacket she'd bought specially for the morning, the softness of the color made her shake. Pale blue, baby blue, little boy blue.

The weather was overcast, a touch too muggy to have pleased Ewan particularly, but at least it wasn't sunny. Will said that was OK. Andrea still wasn't talking much, she let her makeup speak for her. Four thick dark lines sweeping across her upper and lower lids, light mascara, pale face, no blusher, no lipstick. It was a good look. A tight, drawn, cold look. Andrea was feeling pretty cold. Will wouldn't hold her, refused to kiss her, pushed her away the night before even when she tried to offer him a blowjob. Andrea didn't understand and Will couldn't explain. They met at Sally's house and walked the five hundred yards to the church. No one cried. Not then. Crying would have made it too real. Sally's mother wanted to shake her daughter, wrench out the tears. She'd said the day before that if Sally didn't let it out she'd make herself sick. Sally was sick, it didn't make it any better. She and Andrea both reckoned they'd lost half a stone between the fall and the funeral.

Ewan's mum and his big sister, step-sister, were greeting people at the door. His dad was already inside, talking to the vicar, sorting things out. Ewan's mum smiled when they walked up. These were Ewan's friends. His best friends. She liked that they were in black, had defied her ruling. She liked that they still had spirit. Mrs. Stirling hoped Ewan still had spirit, but didn't know for sure. She kissed them all, and then his step-sister Emma did too. Because her mother told her to, because apparently it was what she was supposed to do, stand at the door of a church she'd only ever been to half a dozen times before, waiting for the car that was bringing her little brother in a cherry-wood coffin that seemed way too big for him.

There were a lot of people to get in, loads of kids from school, kids who hardly even knew Ewan, Daniel reckoned, they just wanted a morning off, and a bunch of parents too. Will's dad came, Daniel and Sally's mothers, one or two teachers, no doubt sent to check that everyone who'd said they were going to the funeral really had gone. Eventually the vicar—who Daniel said was a priest, Sally didn't know what the difference was—asked them all to stand and the family walked up the aisle behind Ewan's coffin. Sally had never been into this church. Her own mum went to church a bit more than Ewan's family; Sally went with her every now and then, but her mum's church was plainer, cooler. White walls, clear windows, and the ceiling was lower—this one went too far up. And there was so much happening, stained glass windows, statues and over-full vases, pollen and incense. This church had too much going on. The church Sally went to didn't have a dead Jesus either, up there on his cross, broken and bloody and bent. Given the circumstances, it was a fairly insensitive pose.

The priest said nice things, wrong things, things Ewan's family probably wanted to hear. About him being good at school and a popular student and having some special friends—he looked at them when he said that and Andrea started crying. He said about Ewan wanting to be a doctor, except that he said Ewan wanted to be a GP like his father and even Ewan's dad knew that wasn't really true. But Dr. Stirling was happy to hear it, happy for other people to hear it. Emma talked about her little brother, told some stories about when she was small and he was just new. Her voice shaking, biting her lip at the end of each careful sentence so she didn't start crying. Not yet, not until after the good words. His uncle did a reading. Then the priest came back and talked some more about mysterious ways and many rooms. Sally had heard these stories before and she thought how lucky the priest was that he got to say things people already knew, words they'd learned in RE or had heard in other churches. Already knowing them made the words sound comforting, like they might be real. And then he commended Ewan's body to God. Sally hoped there was a God. Hoped Ewan got to keep going. She wasn't sure though.

They didn't go back to the house and they didn't go for a drink later that evening with some of the other kids from their class, they didn't go back to any of their own places either. They went off, separately, one by one. Andrea asked Will to come back to hers but he said no. He went home with his dad. None of them ever talked about the funeral.

That evening, in bed, Sally remembered how the priest had also kept saying Ewan was a pure soul. He'd said it a couple of times. She figured he meant Ewan was a virgin. And that perhaps his parents had wanted him to say so, to let people know. But then she also wondered about that, because when they were leaving, saying goodbye, trying to avoid Ewan's mum and dad, she'd heard Emma crying to her mate, about the things Ewan didn't get to do. The things he hadn't done yet and now wasn't ever going to do, and how terrible that was. Sally wondered if she should have told them.

172

That Ewan had said all along he wasn't a virgin, had told them all about that girl in France, but even if he'd been lying about her—and Sally thought maybe he had been lying, maybe he would have been more in control yesterday if the French girl had really happened—but anyway, he wasn't a virgin now, definitely not. So he had done that, and it had been OK. Sally thought it had been OK, good enough, better than what her sister had said. It had been all right. For him. And for her. So they didn't need to mind about that, maybe he was a pure soul. Sally didn't know what it took to have a pure soul, but Ewan wasn't a virgin, he had done that. Maybe it was one thing they didn't need to mind so much. But Sally didn't say anything. Just in case. In case they didn't want to know. Or in case they asked for her to tell them more.

THIRTY-FIVE

These places, when Janine had seen them on TV, were always white. And quiet. Calm. But not here. Janine walked through a wide room and was surprised by the noise. A TV in this corner, a radio in that, another room with people shouting at each other, play-shouting, it was a game, but it was still noisy. And there were no cool white walls. These walls were pale green, mostly, except where they were scuffed, and the repeated broken corners where a tea trolley had been carelessly wheeled, taken out chunks of plaster, each uneven corner level with the last. There was a smell of old food and stewed tea, clean sheets, and something acid underneath, piss maybe. It was a warm smell, not entirely unpleasant, like an old lady and a baby were sharing a bedroom. They walked further along, she and the two nurses who held her arms lightly and talked over her head to each other.

Through the next door, down a long wide corridor, double-glazed windows on one side and half a dozen paintings on the other. One of the nurses explained them to Janine, she said the paintings were quite new and the other one pointed out that, all the same, the bright light through the sealed windows had faded them already. And maybe that was just as well she added, over Janine's head again, the attempt at inclusion passed on.

Janine looked at the paintings as they passed. She'd liked art classes when she was younger, when she first went to the grammar school. They'd talked about public art in class once, a visiting artist came and told them about making art accessible to the people. He said that meant getting it on hospital walls and in the loos at King's Cross Station. He showed them slides of his work and the other kids thought it was funny that there should be paintings on the wall of the loo. A couple of the boys reckoned they'd have really good pissing contests if they had art in their toilets, ten points if you hit the Mona Lisa's smile. The artist didn't like the boys. He talked to Janine though, gave her a card of his work. She kept it on her dressing table for two years. Janine didn't know if these paintings on the walls were good art or not. All the people in them looked sick. Maybe that was right, maybe they were meant to look sick, it was hospital art. Janine thought she would have preferred happy pictures, smiling faces. These faces looked like they were telling the stories that made them cry. Janine tried to tell her story but the words came out as noise and tears dried up her mouth. Wasn't that weird? All the tears that were pouring out of her eyes, even when she closed her eyes, even when she tried to sleep, all those so wet tears dried her up. She opened her mouth and nothing came out. Her tongue stuck to the roof of her mouth, teeth barred the way of sentences and she had nothing to say. They walked on past pale green walls.

Will Gallagher left school at the end of that year, went on a TV presenting course and when that didn't work he went on to drama school, his dad paying more than he could afford, more than he wanted to, Will promising to pay him back one day. Which he did. When he graduated he was Ross. Ross Gallagher was even more attractive and lovable than Will had been, he perfected the classic role—dangerous rogue, charming rascal, the one she can't help loving, no matter what he says or does, because underneath it all, she's sure there's a heart of pure gold just waiting to be held and loved, ready and waiting to love her back. He studied at a drama school where they prided themselves on their ability to break kids down and then build them up again. One year to dismantle all the coping mechanisms they'd proudly garnered by eighteen, another year to experiment and find out who they really were, a third year to bring together the new self, honest self, whole self—just in time for the casting directors and agents to get a good long look at the re-created product. That they regularly dumped half the class before the end of the second year tended not to be advertised a great deal—the ones they couldn't break or couldn't rebuild generally didn't make it as far as the graduation performances. Will Gallagher, however, willingly took himself apart, studied his dark places in the open group of his drama school year, exposed himself to the brutal gaze of tutors and fellow students alike, and then remade himself as Ross. And if the reigning tutors couldn't tell that he was hiding his truly dark places, that what he showed them was partial penumbra, not proper eclipse, it didn't stop them fancying him. Will fucked three of the girls in his class, a new one each year, two of the dance and movement tutors, and just the one visiting TV director, a bloke. The school usually frowned on student-teacher relationships, but an attractive straight boy choosing to fuck an older gay man was seen as a good sign. Ross was clearly willing to delve deep into his true self—while discovering a quick route to grabbing his first agent and his first proper job. He cornered the market in tough-youth-with-vulnerable-heart, later graduating to bastard-made-good. Eventually. With the love of a good woman. And his agent gave him the chance to throw in the occasional irredeemable bastard, just to keep them wanting, show his versatility.

After a while, words came back to Janine. Good morning and good night were easy. Yes please, thank you. She was polite, nice. Helpful. The drugs were heavy at first and they slowed her down, her walk, her talk. That was OK really, Janine didn't mind the lack of speed. Things had been going too fast for a while and slow was good, it worked for her, gave her time to think, to sort things out, to make the leaps from one thought to another. In time Janine attended one-on-one therapy, group therapy, art therapy, which she loved and drama therapy, which she thought was a load of crap where the tutors showed off more than the patients. She talked about her childhood and her brothers and her mum and dad. She talked about primary school and secondary school and how she'd never really managed to fit in, not since starting big school. She talked about being picked on in class and about being hassled in the playground, about home being safe and quiet and how she liked it when her mum and dad were working and her big brother was away and her little brother was out and she was just by herself. When the time came, she went to court and did as they told her, answered the barristers' questions, spoke slowly and carefully to the judge, listened to her doctor and the social worker, and didn't mind when her mum started crying and had to be led out of the room. Did mind, didn't show it. She answered all their questions as best she could and tried to do the right thing. She didn't understand everything they were asking her, but she tried. The drugs slowed her down and the words were thick in her head, too wide for her mouth. She went back to the hospital and her group and her doctor and she became used to the fading art on the walls and the warm smell of tea and wee and time passed. She said lots of things but she never told anyone about what had happened with Sally and she never talked about that night and she never told anyone what she'd been trying to say that morning, thought she'd said that morning, hadn't said that morning.

Andrea Browne stayed on at school when Will left, stayed on with Will during the early part of his transition to Ross, but they broke up after his second drama school shag—the second he'd told her about—breaking his own rules about not fucking around and breaking them big. Then she counted the days until she could leave home. After the break-up Andrea said she didn't want to bother with any of the other boys at school, after Will Gallagher there wasn't much point. At least not in having any official boyfriend, anyone she admitted to, gave all her time to. She turned to the other side of Andrea—concentrated solely on her studies, becoming the class star her teachers had always said she could be, but had never thought possible as long as personal biology pulled her away from the book variety. At university, Andrea discovered she could have it all, mostly without ever becoming fully sober. She worked hard, played hard, drank hard, drugged hard, shagged hard. Anyone she could find. For three full years. She left with a First, a cocaine lust, and a surprise gift fiancé: he asked, she said yes, surprising herself as well as him. Then the fiancé became a husband, a carefree honeymoon became their first baby, and before she had worked out what she could possibly do with a degree in Humanities, Andrea was a fully-fledged wife and mother. One more baby and she was still unhappy, not actively searching, but inactively pining. When the teenage sex goddess of a small suburban pond becomes wife and mother to a city banker's family, there's only so much compensation that can be derived from the husband's pay packet. As early twenties shadowed into late, Andrea's husband's best mate, Robert, offered his undying love as an alternative and she leapt at his offer. Wild child to Stepford Wife to Wicked Lady. And when she discovered that the new life with Robert offered the hope of redemption as well as escape, Andrea's sins were washed away in the blood of her broken marriage. One more baby with Robert and the conversion was complete—a trinity of children lifted her from whore to Virgin. In public at least. As long as she remembered to keep on praying. And keep her secrets.

Janine left the hospital and moved home with her mum and dad. She had another bad time when her mum died and went back to the hospital for a bit. A different ward this time, pale peach walls and no paintings. She wasn't there for long and when she was ready to leave her dad explained that it was time she had a place of her own. Her dad had a girlfriend, he needed space. Janine was more surprised that he no longer needed her mum, but didn't say so. Her key worker at the hospital found her a halfway house and she moved in there. The walls were brown and yellow, old wallpaper and painted floorboards. Janine had a front door key of her own and a part-time job with the charity that owned the house and responsibility for the upstairs bathroom, the one the women shared. She very nearly had a proper boyfriend too, but then Nicholas had one psychotic episode too many and the trustees said he was no longer safe to stay in the house and he had to move on. They kissed goodbye and she cried for three days. After that, talking seemed kind of pointless again and Janine's words faded away. She stuck to the basic combinations of yes, no, please, and thank you. It was easier that way.

Daniel Carver made new friends, easier friends. Friends where he was the special and important one. Friends in the years younger than him, people who had not seen Ewan fall, who did not know Ewan though they'd heard his name. Daniel Carver discovered that girls, especially those in the year or two below him at school, wanted to hear his stories in a way that Will and Andrea and Sally and Ewan never really had. He told them all about how close he and Ewan had been, what good times they'd had, how long they had known each other, and how very much he'd lost when he lost his best mate. He discovered a tragic hero was something to be.

When Daniel left school he transported himself to Australia for a girl and a film production course. Neither lasted, though the girl was dumped sooner than the course. Then he tried America, where he discovered a British accent to be exceptionally useful in chatting up young ladies, and quite useful for larger tips while waiting on tables, waiting for his break. He took a part-time film degree, a scriptwriting course, made three low budget films with a dozen mates. And then, just like that, he had his hit. Surprise hit, shock hit, overnight indie and underground success, morphing into big-time possibilities—none of which Daniel actually had the skills to follow up on—followed swiftly by overnight fall. He grew a little older and his bald patch appeared and as the days since his success lengthened, home became ever more attractive. The education system welcomed him with open arms and a full grant to study teacher training for a year—English Literature, Drama, and Film Studies. And then he went back to the area where Ewan had died, houses were cheaper round there, his mother made him dinner every now and then, he'd always been a star in her eyes. He found a nice, quiet pub. The original entrance to the old school had been demolished nine years earlier; in its place was a Portakabin class-room for the new refugee kids who spoke almost no English but had to go somewhere. The local authority thought a Portakabin would just about do. The local kids were adept at taking the piss in a variety of eastern European accents. Daniel Carver didn't get on too well with his fellow teachers, they weren't all that interested in his stories of world travel and the New York film scene. The students, on the other hand, thought he was quite cool. In an aging-letch sort of way.

When the halfway house had to close because of funding problems Janine stayed with her father for a month until her new stepmother kindly and carefully explained that it was all very well, but they had a life of their own now, and Janine must understand there simply wasn't room—after all, she was a grown woman, surely she wanted a place of her own, a life of her own. She went to stay with her little brother for an even shorter time, but he was living in a shared house himself and there simply wasn't space for Janine. Not when she couldn't be bothered to make conversation with his flatmates, lay on the sofa all day. They had proper jobs. If she was going to stay the least she could do was make herself useful.

Janine did like the idea of being useful, only she wasn't sure how to do it. She wondered about going to Germany to see her big brother, still in the army, still sending a card every Christmas and birthday. But the wondering turned to confusion and Janine couldn't work out where to be next, how to be next. Too long in a place where they looked after her and she made none of her own choices, too long not knowing what she would choose if she were asked. Another month and it was warm spring and easy to be on the street anyway. Light and cool, and she found her way to a school, hung around the gates a while. The gates were higher now, the fence bigger. Some of the kids laughed at her, one or two threw coins, that was nice of them. A teacher came out once and asked her what she wanted, said she really couldn't stay there. Janine was fine until they threatened the police and then she stayed away from the school in the daytime, only went there to sleep. Spring nights with showers followed by cool clear skies, sleeping facing the stars and the deep orange sky.

Then they shut up the school for the Easter break and the kids were really happy and no one came to ask Janine to move on and the buildings were all closed and yet that Portakabin was so easy to get into. And Janine Marsden was back in a school with no one else there, in the easy dark, behind the walls and high chain-link fences. The wide playground was all hers. All that space, all that silence. She liked it there.

Sally left school as soon as she could persuade her parents to let her and had a succession of boring jobs. Then she had a succession of interesting jobs. None of them appealed enough to stay with them. She signed on and signed off. She drank too much for a while, drank too little for another while, had a major heartbreak. And another. Then another. Carrie was the worst. She was celibate for a while—intentionally. She began to work for herself. She had good friends and ex-lovers who became good friends. She met Molly and they fell in love and had a baby. And if it had been hard work being Sally, it was mostly all right being Saz.

THIRTY-SIX

I'm excited now, scared but excited. I've been longing to see you all. I'm truly touched you've made the effort. You see, even though none of this was really my idea, even though—like everything else—it's become bigger than I meant, there is something I want to say.

THIRTY-SEVEN

They went to Will's home. An unmarked off-street entrance and a non-smiling, perfectly beautiful housekeeper in pencil skirt and zip-fronted shirt, who showed them through one big white sitting room into another, almost identical but for the slightly softer shade of nearly-white. Saz figured Will was paying the housekeeper for the privilege of not having her wish them a pleasant day. Or a pleasant anything. The young woman asked what they wanted to drink, nodded as each one spoke, and then turned on her heel and stalked off. Off-white walls, off-white carpets, off-white sofas. As Daniel whispered once she was out of ear-shot, "Nice decor. All Janine needs to feel right at home is a padded cell."

The über-cool housekeeper came back with drinks and told them that Ross would be down shortly. She was going out, wouldn't be back until the evening, anything else they wanted, they'd have to help themselves. She didn't seem too happy about leaving, or the idea that strangers might go through what she clearly viewed as her own place, but apparently she also had no choice. Will came in and glared at her.

"Still here, Anna?"

"No. Gone already."

She left, slamming the front door behind her.

Daniel smiled, "So hard to get the staff these days, isn't it?"

It was one-thirty. Janine was due at two. She didn't arrive. Two-ten came and went, and two-fifteen. Will drank whisky, cutting heavily into the new bottle Anna had opened; Daniel stuck to iced water. Neither Saz nor Andrea wanted anything. Until two-twenty-five, when Will poured more whisky and the other three started on the wine. Will was the most obviously nervous, pacing the tiled floor, checking his mobile, his watch, the TV for local news, the radio for tube and traffic reports. He went to and from the kitchen half a dozen times, bringing back more bottles of water than they could possibly need. By two-thirty he was furious.

"This is ludicrous. Stupid bitch. She's probably got the wrong fucking street, got lost because she's too much of a loser to find her way here."

"Mmm. Or she's just not coming. Have you thought of that?" Andrea was tired of Will's anger. "Maybe she's having a laugh at our expense."

"I know what she said when we spoke yesterday. I'm not an idiot. She was perfectly serious."

Andrea pushed her mouth muscles into a version of a smile. "Or maybe she's only laughing at you. For an actor you don't hide your feelings very well, do you?"

"What?"

"You're making this into such a big deal, Will. Calm down."

Will Gallagher wasn't having that. "Piss off, Andrea, it is a big deal. If Janine Marsden goes to the tabloids with her story, you'll be in as much shit as me. Maybe not public shit, but you might have a few tricky questions to answer to your husband—second, is it, or third? I mean, I know it's not as if any of you have a career." He looked around the room at the three of them, warming to his theme now. "Clearly it's my living that's on the line as well as my relationship, but I don't think any of you can pretend this doesn't matter. Or you wouldn't be here, would you?"

"Yeah," Daniel countered, "As you say, none of us is the huge success you are, Will. None of us is planning to sell our wedding photos so they can be displayed in doctors' waiting rooms for all time. You're so amazing. Which we all know. Have done for years. But you said Janine wanted to see all of us, right? Well, here we are. You may think you're the most important person here, but clearly Janine doesn't. And for a mad bitch, that makes pretty good sense."

Will sat down, drank a deep mouthful of his whisky. Daniel

smiled, pleased with himself for putting their case so clearly, grinned at Andrea, hoping for her praise. She ignored him and picked up the phone to call Robert, telling him she'd be home on a later train than they'd planned.

Saz looked around the room. They were such an odd group. In retrospect they probably always had been, but it hadn't seemed so obvious when they were younger, orbiting around the whims of Will Gallagher, pulled this way by Andrea's moods, pushed in another direction by Daniel trying to usurp Will, she and Ewan struggling to keep up, juggling each other for fourth or fifth position. The dynamic they had all put up with in the past no longer held them so tightly. Andrea didn't need Will Gallagher's attention. She knew she was a good-looking woman, the years had simply added to her attractiveness, and the fact that she no longer seemed to need the men to fancy her made her still lovelier. Meanwhile Will's current fear diminished his past status, and his nerves left him looking physically worn. While he looked great on TV, in the flesh he was slightly too thin, his lack of body fat scratched the worry lines deeper into the lightly tanned skin of his face. Certainly he had the public kudos and wallet to match, but in this room, at this moment, Will was weaker than she'd ever seen him. Daniel, on the other hand, looked the most comfortable of all of them. Certainly she'd never before seen him revel so blatantly in Will's discomfort, but then she knew there were other secrets Daniel wasn't yet telling. For her part Saz just wanted to get it all over with.

They were quiet for a few minutes then, while Will checked his answerphone, his agent, and then another answer service in case there were any other calls he'd missed. There were none. And Janine Marsden was forty-five minutes late.

Andrea looked up from the glossy coffee-table book she was studying. "It's probably some stupid tube strike they've just decided on for no good reason, or a taxi that refused to go north of the river or whatever. I am so glad I don't live here anymore."

Saz said, "You used to love the city. When we were kids all you went on about was moving further in and higher up."

"True. But I was misguided, I didn't yet know how ghastly London is. And dirty. And badly managed."

"Shut up, Andy." Will was with Saz on this one. "I get so sick of you people who move out, as if your country idyll isn't paid for by Londoners' taxes, by the people who are prepared to keep on working here, by the people who can't afford to sell up and sell out like you."

"Yeah, Will, you certainly understand selling out. And I'm sure you really know so many of the little people, the ones who really matter. When was the last time you even went on the tube?"

Will smiled, he could do this, he might be at the end of his tether over Janine Marsden's late arrival, he might be finding Daniel's apparent calm unnerving, but he could always put Andrea Browne in her place. "Fuck off, babe, you've always wanted to be what you're not. You wanted to be the best lay in school, when we were sixteen, yes? But guess what? Telling everyone that was the case didn't actually make it true. And now you've turned into this English rose parody—and sure, the soft pastels really suit you, as if you didn't know—but pretending to be the vicar's wife doesn't actually make it your truth."

"Very nice."

"Very true. I'm just suggesting you take a look at who you really are."

"Happy to, as long as you'll take a look at yourself. We're all here because you're terrified that Janine Marsden is going to expose you for what you were back then. And maybe even still are. But while the rest of us might be able to deal with a few home truths, this wonderful life of yours couldn't possibly accommodate reality. So don't start with me, because if anyone knows quite what a bastard you are, I do."

Eventually Daniel broke the silence, "Ah, look, if you two want to go upstairs … sort this out between you? I'm sure Saz and I will be fine for fifteen minutes? Twenty?"

Saz rounded on him. "It's not funny, Daniel. We're all dealing with some horrible stuff from way back."

186

"Actually, I think it's hilarious. You know, like those jokes we used to play on each other? The nasty interaction that passed for friendship back then, when Will always came out on top? Just like he's trying to win now. See if he can't shout louder than Andrea, flash more money around than me, play a more all-knowing twat than you ..."

"Thanks," Saz spat back.

"You're welcome. And he always thinks he knows better than anyone else, don't you, Will? I guess that's experience for you. Will Gallagher getting what he wants, when he wants it, how he wants it. Well, almost always. Once or twice we might have been a little busy to think about you." He turned to Andrea. "Eh, Andy?"

Andrea had a sharp intake of breath at his words and it turned into a cold laugh, a shake of her head. "You're good at this, aren't you, Daniel? Fucking people over, twisting the knife?"

"Years of practice. Years of working out how not to come second. Or at least, to maybe look like I was coming second, but to try and win anyway."

Will looked up from his still silent mobile phone. "What are you on about? At what point, Daniel, in your very ordinary life, have you ever done better than second? If that? Oh, other than your one big success of course—how long ago was it now? Five years? Ten?"

Daniel smiled. Lifted his wine glass to his mouth. "I don't know, Will. Maybe the time I was fucking your girlfriend behind your back? Like pretty much most of the time that you were going out with her while we were at school? When she just couldn't decide if you really were as brilliant a shag as you said you were? If she didn't fancy someone who might have been a little less pretty, but a whole lot brighter?"

They were silent then. Andrea looked at her hands, twisting her wide wedding ring, the men glaring at each other. Saz thought they might actually start to physically fight and she wasn't at all sure she'd be able to stop them if they did. Or if she could be bothered to.

Then Will smiled. "And did you think she was the best fuck in the school? I taught her as well as I could, you know."

Andrea shrunk further back into the big armchair, humiliated by both men and the desperation of her teenage self. And Saz watched as Will seemed to grow in stature; not giving in to Daniel's revelation gave him the strength he'd been lacking. But it was watching Daniel that encouraged her to speak. The old Daniel Carver would have backed down eventually. Made a joke about Andrea, would have wanted to maintain at least a semblance of an alliance with Will. But he didn't. Saz knew Daniel had more still.

"I think there's something else going on here. I think you know something, Daniel, something you haven't told us yet. To do with Janine?"

THIRTY-EIGHT

Saz had to hand it to him, Daniel was cooler than she would ever have given him credit for. He looked at her over the rim of the wine glass he'd been holding to his lips for the past hour—holding she now noticed but, unlike the rest of them, certainly unlike Will with the whisky, barely sipping from.

"I don't know what you're talking about, Sally."

"Yeah, you do. Becky told me."

"You saw her again?"

"This morning, on my way here. You fucked up, Daniel, you should have known better than to think she wouldn't put out for a higher bidder. Or wouldn't mind when she knew about you and Andrea."

Will turned back from his view, head shaking, glass empty. "Why would the girl care about Daniel and Andrea before she was even born?"

Saz sighed. "You really don't get it, do you? God, if it wasn't all such a fucking mess, I think I'd quite enjoy seeing you like this, Will."

Then she told them about Daniel and Andrea. And Daniel and Janine.

"What the fuck?"

"I don't understand."

"You and Daniel? Andrea—surely not? You and Daniel? All this time? Seriously?"

"You've seen Janine?"

"Why would you do this to us?"

Daniel had seen Janine Marsden at the school gates before the

189

Easter break, before he'd had to leave the school himself. He didn't recognize her at first, saw a few of the kids giving her a hard time and told them to leave it out, give the old lady a break. And when he came closer, saw she wasn't an old lady at all. And when he came closer still, he thought maybe he knew her from somewhere. It was the middle of the night when he remembered where from. He didn't get back to sleep again that night. Gave her five quid the next day and had a word with the Head about the woman who was causing a nuisance at the east gate. And Janine was grateful for the money, though he didn't think she knew who he was. And then there was the fuss when they found her staying in the Portakabin after the holidays; Becky told him about it, and Daniel had an idea. He went one night when the school was empty, found the woman and talked to her. It took a little while but he persevered. And she remembered him and eventually, after some time, after he'd helped her to find a place, Janine Marsden made a leap of faith and agreed with Daniel that it was time they all met up again, had a reunion. She made the first phone call to Will from Daniel's flat.

"My God, Daniel, but you're a cunt."

Will launched himself at Daniel and the two men started beating up on each other. Taking it and giving it, punch-bag bodies both. Saz and Andrea moved away from them into the adjoining sitting room, the shuttered doors between the two rooms open. They sat on the fat white sofa.

Andrea spoke first. "Do you want to do anything?"

Saz watched Will smash his fist into the back of Daniel's head. "About them?"

"Yeah."

"No. I don't think so." Will's nose was bleeding, dark red down his white shirt and slippery on the spotless floor tiles. "I hate all this minimalist crap. It'll look better when they're done."

When they were done was only another five minutes. Andrea looked around the room, the two men both bleeding a little, both bruised a lot, each collapsed into a fat armchair. The padded writing table and chrome standard lamp were lying on their sides, spooning each other. "And there I was thinking we were all the best of old friends. Feel better now?"

Will's answer was swift, his voice thickened by his swollen mouth. "Yeah. He's been asking for it."

"You've been asking for it," Daniel answered, stirring from his chair.

"We've all been asking for it," Andrea said.

Saz shook her head, it was all too familiar, she and Andrea watching from the sidelines while the boys fought it out. "I can't believe this is what you're pissed off about. It's like you don't even feel bad about all that, what happened to Janine."

"You know nothing about how I feel, Saz. You don't know how any of us feels," Will mumbled through his cut lip.

"OK, but I admit I've felt crap about all this for ages."

Andrea answered her. "And you think the rest of us haven't?"

"That's not what I'm saying." Though Saz did feel the other woman had touched on something of her truth, and her next words were harsher because of it. "We should have said something then."

"Like what?" Daniel asked. "Would you have told the cops the whole story, or just the bit that put some of us in the shit and not you? Because it's all joined up. Everything that happened, everything you did that led to what we did that led to what she did."

"For fuck's sake," Will interrupted, his voice clearer with the effort to get his point across, "we were so off our faces half the time back then, I'm not even sure I remember it clearly anyway, that night or any of the others."

"I do," Andrea said quietly.

"No, hold on, let's just check this out," Daniel spoke over her. "Sally wishes she'd told the whole truth back then. Is that right?"

"I think so."

"Oh, right, you 'think so' now? Because half a minute ago you were certain we were totally wicked, while you were more or less blame-free. You really think if you'd told the whole story that you'd have felt better about what happened to Ewan?"

"I don't know."

"Yeah, well I do," Daniel answered. "Will's right. Some of the stuff we all got up to was bloody rough. Not just the shit about Janine, but the drugs and the drinking, and the sex. Stupid fucked-up teenage shit. Some of it was just taking the piss and some of it was well and truly illegal. And I'm really not sure you'd have been able to work out which bits to tell and which not. And that's why none of us said anything."

"Yeah," Saz agreed, "and why all of us have been feeling crap about it for so long."

"Maybe." Daniel nodded at Will, slumped in his chair, "I don't think Will's thought about it at all. I think he left us lot behind and was perfectly happy to do so. He never paid the rest of us any proper attention."

Andrea was incredulous. "Is that what all this was about? Having a go at Will because you want his attention? Because you're jealous? Bloody hell, Daniel, if that's your reasoning for bringing up all this shit again, then you're fucking madder than Janine."

Daniel shrugged, clearly confused. "I don't know. There's us as well. You and me ..."

Will looked up, "Yeah, let's hear all about Andrea and Daniel."

Andrea ignored him, glaring at Daniel, "Please don't say you did it for me, that really would be taking the piss."

"I didn't not do it for you."

"What does that mean?"

"You've always wanted Will. And hated him. Way back since we were kids you've felt like that. Even when you and I were fucking behind his back, all that time, he was always the one you cared about."

Saz interrupted, "But, Daniel, why didn't you tell us you knew Andrea when Will and I met up with you two weeks ago? Why the Aunty Jane story? Or was that all just part of your game?"

Andrea answered for him. "That's probably down to me. I didn't want anyone to know we still saw each other. I made him promise ages ago."

Saz was stunned. "And that's the one promise he decides to keep? Incredible."

"So you two have been shagging all this time?" Will was laughing at them. "You really are a mess, Andy."

Andrea rubbed her hands over her face. "We've seen each other on and off. There were times when I saw Daniel as—I don't

192

know—an escape maybe, from the life I've got myself into. But, you know, I never made the leap to him either. He's right, I did always have a thing about you. An unresolved thing." She sighed. "Feels like maybe it's over now."

"Lucky me, and so he's been using Janine to blackmail me to prove his undying love for you?"

Andrea held up her hands. "I have no idea. Daniel?"

Daniel was fingering his cut eye, rubbed the red and swollen knuckles of his right hand. "It just all got carried away. I knew you were unhappy in the country, with Robert."

Andrea shrugged. "I'm not satisfied, I've never been satisfied. I don't think I ever will be. That's hardly news; I didn't realize you thought you needed to rescue me."

"I wanted to help."

"I didn't ask for your help."

"No, I know." Daniel agreed, as if that was part of his problem. "But I tried to speak to Will about it. See if we could do anything for you. God knows, he's got more than enough cash. He could have done something for you, you could have started again."

"Again again, you mean." Andrea shook her head. "And no, I couldn't. One failed marriage is enough for me, thank you. I'll put up with this one. But even if I was going to leave Robert, I certainly wouldn't take Will's money to get away."

Andrea and Daniel looked at each other for understanding and found mutual incomprehension.

Will spoke up, "What are you on about, Daniel? You were never in touch with me."

Daniel nodded. "I was. I left messages with your agent. I sent a letter. I left a note when you did some charity show in town."

"And you think I actually get that shit passed on to me?"

"Maybe. Anyway, then I got your number."

"How?"

"Some website groupie thing. This old lady sold it to me. She got it off a journalist. Cost me three hundred quid."

"You paid for my phone number? So why the fuck didn't you just call me?"

And as he shouted, Will finally realized Daniel had called.

193

Remembered coming home, listening to the message and then wiping it that night, not interested.

"You should have called back."

"Maybe. I don't think you'd have listened anyway. And I was pissed off. And then I found Janine at the school, and I did help her, found her a place to stay, got her off the street. We talked a bit—she's still pretty confused—but she remembers you, Will. And she certainly remembers Sally. It just started out as a gag, I was going to call you afterwards and tell you the truth, honest. I thought perhaps we could try and do something for Janine. I mean, it's not all our fault she was living on the street, but ... well, we are part of it."

Daniel was asking for understanding for his actions, Saz just wanted him to get on with it. "So why didn't you call Will back and explain?"

"He got scared. Really scared." Daniel turned to Will. "I was listening to Janine talking to you and I could hear your voice on the other end of the line and you were totally freaked. At first I thought maybe we could just get you to give us some money, I'd pass some on to Andrea and she could leave Robert, I'd help Janine get herself sorted out ..."

"Christ, you really think you're some kind of savior, don't you? Saving me, saving Janine," Andrea spat at him. "And if Will had given you money for me, what do you think I'd have done with it? Run away with you?"

"Maybe. You might as well be dissatisfied with me as with anyone else. Anyway, that's not what happened. The one time I tried to talk to you about leaving Robert, you went off at me and then I was pissed off at you too, and I figured I'd give this a go instead. See if I could do it. Freak you all out."

Saz stared at Daniel, stunned. "And does it feel good?"

Daniel looked around at the three of them, his old school friends. Saz shaking with a combination of shock and fury, Will bleeding from the cut on his lip, his nose swollen and bloody, Andrea's eyes red with tears. "I suppose I'm meant to say no, it wasn't worth

194

it. But you know what? You three have always been so fucking arrogant—you too, Andrea, you were never happy with any of your blokes, but you never even thought about taking me seriously—you all always thought I was a bit weird, not as good looking as Will, not cute like Ewan. You never took my work or my ambitions seriously. The one-hit wonder, always just not quite it. So yeah, actually, this does feel good. In a way. I really got you. All of you."

THIRTY-NINE

Silence. A car horn beeped outside, and another, a third, muffled by the careful double glazing. London carried on outside. The room was too warm. Saz was shattered.

"So what now?" Will was slumped in his seat, no longer making any attempt to deny his exhaustion or lack of sobriety.

Andrea stood up, picked up her bag. "Nothing. It's all said and done. Janine clearly has more sense than the rest of us. We've given her an hour and a half. She's not coming. I shouldn't have either."

Daniel stood up, held his hand out to her, "Andrea?"

"Finished, Daniel." She looked around at the others, "Let's not do this again."

"But what about Janine?" Saz asked.

"Apparently you're the one with the big guilt, Sally, you sort her. I'm going home. I won't be seeing any of you again. I won't be talking about any of this again. Goodbye."

Will waited until the door closed behind her and then shifted himself painfully from his chair to the sofa. "She's right, it's all done now. You had your fun, Daniel, time to run off home to your boring ordinary life now."

"Don't push me, Will. I could still talk about this, you know …"

Will kicked off his shoes, punched a cushion behind his head. "Yeah, you could. And you could talk about your part in whatever happened to Janine, how you used her back then and you've used her again now. Taking a woman off the streets and trying to involve her in a blackmail scam? Nice. Or perhaps you'd like to talk about this kid you've been shagging, that'll look great on your CV. Or maybe you just want to write it all up and turn it into a screenplay? Your terribly interesting life?" He ran a hand carefully over his face. "Like Andrea said, it's finished. Fuck off, mate. I'm going to sleep. Let yourselves out, yeah?" He lay down, turned onto his side away from them and closed his eyes.

Saz picked up her bag with shaking hands, checked for her phone. At the front door she turned to Daniel and said, "You're not the only one."

"Only one what?"

"You said Will thought he was better than you. But I felt like that too, about Andrea, about loads of people. Always did. Felt like I didn't belong, couldn't keep up with everyone else, that you were all judging me. And I know Ewan felt it, we talked about it once. I bet Andrea did too, even though she'd never say, not then, probably not even now." She lowered her voice. "That's why we found each other. Because we didn't fit with the others and being together gave us somewhere to hide. But that's not a big deal, Daniel. No one ever thinks they belong, not when they're kids, not when they're adults half the time. We were lonely and scared and fucked up simply because we were kids. That's how it is. It was just safer being lonely and scared in a group."

Daniel ran a careful hand over his battered face. "Nice bit of psychology, Saz. Might even be true for you, and Ewan. Was true some of the time for me, Andrea occasionally. But I don't believe it was true for Will, never has been. He really did think he was better than the rest of us." He looked back at the man stretched out on the big soft sofa. "And he still does. It's why you and I know that we damaged Janine Marsden, and he decided to believe it was all just a good time gone too far. Will Gallagher can't be wrong. He doesn't know how to be."

They went out into the street together. Saz wasn't going to walk away with him, but Daniel held the door for her, laughed at her for suddenly coming over all squeamish now. Asked if she was afraid of him. She was, but she wasn't going to say so. He said goodbye in the street and she nodded her agreement. Before she had crossed the road, Saz was on her mobile calling Carrie; she wanted to hear Matilda's voice. But their home phone and Carrie's mobile were both ringing unanswered. Nor did Carrie respond to the seven increasingly worried texts Saz sent. She kept trying all the way home in the cab. Carrie had never failed to answer her phone. Saz was very cold.

FORTY

"Hi, Janine."

"Hello, Sally. You look good. Well."

"Yeah, I am. Was. You look a bit tired?"

"Drugs. Prescription ones," she added quickly. "They're very aging."

"Right ... well ... how are you?"

Saz spoke very slowly and very carefully.

Janine laughed. "You don't need to talk to me like I'm mad. I mean, I might be—a bit—but it's not the same as being stupid. You can talk normally."

"Then what the fuck are you doing here?" This time Saz shouted. Matilda jumped at the noise and started to grizzle, Carrie grinned and then groaned in pain, Janine winced. "OK, how about somewhere in between?"

Janine was sitting on the edge of the sofa, directly opposite Saz as she stood in the doorway. Matilda was lying on Janine's lap, grizzling just a little as she usually did when she was tired.

Saz took a very small step forward. "It's way past time for Matilda's sleep, Janine. Shall I put her to bed?"

"I said that."

Carrie spoke out the side of her mouth. She was less than three feet to Janine's left against the glass door that opened on to the little balcony. She had taken her shirt off and was holding it to her cheek and chin. The shirt was wet with blood and there was a narrow gash down the right side of Carrie's face. Carrie's beautiful face.

Carrie tried again, slower this time. "Janine wanted to wait until you got home."

"Are you OK?"

Carrie tried to shrug. "Don't know. Still, you're right about it not being boring at home with the kid though."

"Yeah, always plenty to do." Saz's speech was measured, careful, watching Matilda. Her eyes to Carrie. "What …?"

"Don't really know. Told you to put your bottles in the recycling though, didn't I?"

"Sorry."

"Well, remember next time."

Janine was stroking Matilda's thick curls with one hand. In the other, six inches from the baby, she was holding a broken bottle. The wine bottle Saz and Molly had finished the night before. The wine bottle she'd picked up off the back doorstep and smashed across Carrie's head and face when Carrie opened the door.

She smiled at Saz. "Your baby's nice."

"We think so. Can I hold her?"

"No."

"How about you give her to Carrie?"

"No."

They looked at each other then, for a while, quietly. The only sound Matilda's soft whimper as she began to fall asleep, the occasional shudder as another truck rolled past outside.

Saz couldn't stand it and began to speak. "I'm sorry, Janine. I'm so sorry. While we were waiting for you, it all came back, all the stuff I've never been able to forget anyway, and I'm so sorry. It got out of hand, we didn't mean to, I'm sure none of us meant to … it was just … we were young, stupid, we were pissed and stupid and I am sorry. Please can I … please don't hurt her … please?" Holding her arms out for Matilda, trying to explain, placate, make better. Trying not to scream. Trying not to cry. Failing.

Janine wasn't crying. She was very calm. "I thought you'd get here sooner. You stayed ages with them."

"We were waiting for you."

"I got lost."

"You should have called Will. One of us could have come to find you."

"I tried. His phone was engaged all the time."

"Not all the time."

"When I called it was engaged."

"He was calling his agent, his manager, everybody. He thought you'd have left him a message. You could have left a message? We'd have come to meet you."

"I don't like leaving messages. They scare me. And I don't have a phone of my own anyway, I was in a phone box and this woman was waiting to use it. She wanted me to move out so she could use it. I think I might have made a fuss. There were cars beeping and carrying on when I left. She was horrible. Mean to me. Anyway, after that I didn't want to see you all together. Not really."

"So how did you know to come here?"

"Daniel gave me your address. I was going to come here yesterday, when you had coffee. He said you were all having coffee?"

"Yeah. We did."

"Well, he wanted me to come then. Surprise you all. Thought it would be really funny. Only I got scared, I couldn't do it. So I rang Will instead, and I meant to come to his house today. I tried. Really."

Carrie shifted against the door, groaned softly, holding the bloody shirt to her face.

Janine looked at Carrie in surprise, registered her sitting there, the blood. "Sorry, that was an accident."

Saz and Carrie spoke at the same time. "Accident?"

"As in I didn't mean to hurt your friend. She said she's not your girlfriend, just friend?"

Saz smiled at Carrie. "Ex-girlfriend, best friend."

Janine nodded. "That's nice. But see, I was really upset when the woman wouldn't let me use the phone box and by the time I'd walked here I'd got furious with you lot, all over again, and I got to your back steps and the bottle was there and it just came out of me when she opened the door." She turned to Carrie. "When you opened the door. I am sorry. You know that, right?" Carrie didn't bother to try to answer. Janine looked back to Saz. "We're all sorry. Aren't we?"

Saz steadied herself against the door jamb. She thought she might throw up.

"I don't know, Janine. Really. I think they are. I know I am. For all of it. The whole fucking lot. But please don't make this any worse. We've lost Ewan …" Then she remembered that Janine had been asking to see all five of them. "Fuck. I mean … oh shit … you know that, don't you? About Ewan? You remember?"

Janine smiled then, a proper smile, pleased with herself. "Of course I knew he was dead, I was just messing with you—I knew it would freak you all. Daniel thought that was really clever of me. And anyway, that's what you think crazy people are like, don't you? You think we don't remember the truth? We can't tell fact from fiction?"

"It did scare us."

"Good."

"Fair enough. Look, Janine, we behaved terribly, and it all went really crazy. I admit that. Absolutely. But this isn't going to make it better. Hurting Carrie and keeping Matilda over there with you, scaring me. We can say sorry, try and make amends somehow, but you doing something else bad is only going to make it worse."

"You think I don't know that? You think I don't know what this looks like? I just want you all to know what really happened."

"I do know, Janine. We talked about it today. We all remembered it today. All of us. We talked about it for the first time. We've never talked about it before."

Janine looked blankly at Saz then. Not understanding, Saz thought she'd said too much, pushed too far. Of course she didn't want to be reminded of that.

Then Janine shook her head. "No. It's not about that. That's not why I agreed when Daniel asked me to call Will. That's not it. Or maybe a bit. Not really. Not the whole thing. That's not it."

Carrie was getting more and more agitated on the floor. "Oh, well what the fuck is it, then?"

Saz wanted to kiss her for speaking back and scream at her for disturbing Janine as she sat with the broken bottle so close to Matilda's soft skin.

She did neither.

Janine brought herself back to the room, this room. Explained.

"Look, I know I was in a bad way that day, really bad. It had been coming for a while, I think. I wasn't OK, I know that. And truthfully, it wasn't just you guys, I think I hadn't been OK for a long time, you were only part of it. A big part of it, the main part of it probably, but only part of it. Anyway, what I mean is, I was there too."

"Where?"

"When Ewan fell."

"And?"

"My point of view was different to yours. Your backs were to the wall—Ewan was in the middle. Will was on one side of him, you were on the other. Daniel and Andrea on the edges. But I was facing all five of you. I saw it all. You only saw me. And from where I was standing I could see each of you, clearly."

"And?"

"And you all let the police and the teachers and everyone else believe I pushed Ewan over the edge."

"No, we didn't, Janine, honest, we never said you meant to do it."

"But I didn't do it."

"What?"

"I didn't do it. I was coming up to talk to you all. I wanted to ask you how you could let that happen, the night before. I wanted to confront you. But that's all. And when I got to the top of the stairs, I saw Will's face. And he was so happy, really getting off on it all. He made me furious. So I lunged at him, at Will. And you thought I was heading for you, and so did Ewan. So Ewan got in the way, between you and me. But that meant he was in Will's way as well. Will wanted to see me, wanted to see what I was going to do. And I promise you, what I wanted to do was push Will Gallagher off the bloody wall, I did want to kill him—just for a moment, but I really did. Only Will pulled Ewan out of the way, grabbed his shirt from behind and pulled him back. Will got to Ewan before I got to either of them. I know it was an accident. Of course he didn't mean to knock him over. But he did. It was Will who pushed Ewan. Not me."

Saz didn't know what to say. It was all horrible, all impossible.

"So what do you want to do now?"

203

Saz looked at Matilda, happy enough on Janine's lap. The broken bottle in Janine's hand.

"I want you to get Will to come over here. I want him to tell the truth."

"Who to?"

"Me. You. Himself. That'll do. I don't care about the cops or any of that shit. I don't trust them anyway. Who's going to believe my word against Will Gallagher's? I just want to hear him say it."

"But you threatened to tell the papers about us. That scared Will, it would fuck up his career, maybe even his marriage."

"I don't care about his bloody career. And if I talked to the newspapers, Will would still deny it. That's not what I want—going to the papers was Daniel's idea, a threat to blackmail him with. Those kind of people have treated me like shit for years, I don't care what the readers of bloody newspapers think. But because I've been thinking about it, because Daniel got me thinking about it, I've worked out that I do care about the truth. And I want to hear it said. Call him."

Saz reached into her bag for her phone and Janine's grip tightened on the bottle. "And Sally?"

"Yes?"

"Dial more than three nines, won't you? Call Will. Not the police. I'm counting."

Will answered his phone on the fifth try. Saz spoke to him quietly, hoping to hide her fear from both Janine and Carrie. She was shocked when Will refused to come over. He sounded drunk and tired and belligerent. She couldn't believe he was refusing her.

"I'll call the cops myself, Will. I'll tell them Janine said all this happened. I'll tell them everything we did, everything you did."

"Right. You'll call the cops that Janine told you not to call? And then what? After she does whatever the fuck she's threatening you with? You'll tell them Janine held a broken bottle to your daughter's face as well as smashing up your mate? You'll ruin Janine's life all over again?"

Will hung up for the third time. When she next called his mobile was turned off, and when she tried the landilne it went immediately to answerphone.

Saz put the phone down. Her legs were trembling so much she thought she might fall over. "I'm sorry, Janine. I can't make him come."

Janine shook her head. "You really do have rubbish friends, don't you?"

Carrie lay watching from the floor.

FORTY-ONE

Carrie had had enough. "OK, look, you two. I've got some idea of what's going on here, but not a lot, that's for sure. Then again, I don't think either of you know much either. You know what? This is really pissing me off, Saz."

"Carrie, shut up, you'll hurt your face."

"Your mate already hurt my face."

"Then shut up because I don't want her to hurt Matilda's face."

"Look, I'm in some degree of pain here, and I've seen enough *ER* and *Casualty* to know that if I don't get my lovely face to a hospital soon, it's going to take a fuck of a lot longer to heal, possibly leaving me scarred and looking like shit for the rest of my young life. Now, call me selfish if you want, but I really don't want that. She's not going to hurt Matilda."

"I might."

"She might."

Saz and Janine spoke at the same time.

"Saz!" Carrie countered. "This is stupid, smacking me round the face like that wasn't an accident, she chose to pick up the bloody bottle, stop being so fucking understanding."

Janine looked down at her. "What's your point?"

"That things get planned. People have ideas, they carry them through. You didn't even know Saz had a baby, you certainly didn't come here meaning to hurt Matilda. You meant to hurt Saz when she came to the door. Violence like this doesn't happen without forethought."

Saz pictured Ewan's body, cracked at the bottom of the concrete wall. "Yeah, it does. That's exactly what happens. It's almost always without forethought. That's why it's so fucking horrible. Surprises are always so shit."

And as she spoke, Saz was nodding. Because she and Carrie knew what they were both talking about, had used arguing with each other as a distraction before, with Molly, with Carrie's other lovers, they had shouted at each other when behind the words they were laughing, making plans, thinking something entirely different.

Carrie was still speaking as she leaped up from the floor, "God, Saz, you're so full of shit sometimes." Still talking as she grabbed Janine's arm holding the broken bottle and wrenched it back over Janine's head. In the same moment Saz crouched down and picked up a stone statue from the fireplace. It was a fat Buddha-shaped woman, heavy and strong in the hips. Carrie had given it to Saz and Molly when they were trying to conceive. She'd said that with belly and thighs that size it just had to be a fertility symbol. Molly had thought it most useful as a doorstop. Saz swung the statue at Janine's stunned face with one arm and lifted Matilda free with the other. Matilda's furious scream rang out over the crack of Janine's jaw.

Saz put out her arm, pushed Janine away, needed her to get away from Matilda, she was still too close, it was all too close. Carrie had hold of Janine's hand, hurting her. Janine pulled away from her, reached for Saz, twisted herself, and then Carrie wasn't helping anymore, and she wasn't in the way anymore, and there was a clear route straight to Saz that Janine was going to take, would take. But Carrie was falling, pulling Janine away from Saz and Matilda and in the fall the broken glass met Carrie's body again. Pushed through skin into flesh into vein. Deep. Across her neck and skewering fresh scars, open flesh, blood pouring out.

Janine slumped down, knocked out with the smash or pain or exhaustion. Saz held her screaming child close to her and tried to grab Carrie with her other arm, hold her up, keep her going. There was hammering on the back door, Saz was shouting for them to come in, to come in and help, whoever it was, just to fucking well come in and help. Then there were three policemen in the room, Will running in behind them, shouting out, "I told you so, I fucking told you we needed to get here sooner." Janine was out cold. And Saz in the middle of the room balancing Carrie and her child. Half of her twisting away, holding Matilda as far from the blood as she could, her other arm dragging Carrie into her, pulling her tight, closer. Carrie was crying, hurting. Saz thought she heard her ask for a kiss, for old time's sake. Carrie's mouth tasted of blood. Only of blood.

They took Carrie to hospital in the ambulance, sirens screaming. But there wasn't much point.

FORTY-TWO

The police took Janine away with them. There was little to say. Saz and Will both played down the past couple of weeks, no one mentioned the blackmail or the phone calls. Neither of them had the stomach for making Janine's life any worse. And for whatever incomprehensible group loyalty reasons, there wasn't much to say about each other either.

By the time Molly arrived home very late that night, Saz felt like she'd been crying for days. She and Matilda were staying with Chris and Marc, had taken some clothes and left the flat as soon as they were allowed. Saz gave Molly a brief account of what had happened and then agreed to explain in more detail later. Molly wasn't ready to hear it yet. While she put off the reasons for Carrie's blood on the lounge floor, Molly told Saz about Asmita, how she'd been, the tears, the horror of watching her mother wailing her loss. And then a walk out in the hills, talking about Ian with some joy as well as pain, the bittersweet of moving on. Saz listened to the mother–daughter story, listened for the signs and accents she'd want to recognize in her own daughter, the depth of child and parent understanding she'd want Matilda to have with her own parents, all of them. Then there was silence and it was time for Saz to speak. She opened her mouth and nothing came out. Tears for Carrie, but no words.

The silence grew and Molly said she'd been thinking about the flat anyway, they needed to talk about moving house. They couldn't go back there now. And they needed somewhere larger, not so nice probably, there was no way they could afford such a great location with a second proper-sized bedroom, let alone the three-bedroom house they'd been coveting for a while now, but a boxroom wasn't going to do Matilda for all that much longer. Molly had spent a few days in her own family home, small house but a huge garden, the trees she'd climbed when she was little, the place she'd hidden in the hedge when Ian and Asmita were the worst parents in the world and Molly was sure she'd probably been adopted. The shops might not be so good wherever they could afford a larger place, the heath not so close, they might need to move further out on the tube line. But it was time to move on.

Saz agreed. It was definitely time to move on.

"Moll, there's stuff I need to tell you. More than just what happened this afternoon."

"Yeah. I didn't think that mad bitch came into our home entirely out of the blue. What about?"

"Me. About me. About what happened, why it happened."

Molly turned over, away from Saz, buried her head into her pillow. "I know about you, Saz."

"No, you don't. There's things I need to tell you."

"Why?"

"What?"

Molly turned back to Saz, looking at her partner though the dark room, the space between them both stretched with lack of light and compacted by the knowing in that space. "Why do you want to tell me things about you?"

"Because you're my partner, because you love me, because we have a child together?"

"That's right. I do. I do love you. But I don't need to know your secrets, Saz. You've always had secrets. I think you've had secrets you didn't even tell yourself, let alone me. And if you didn't want to acknowledge them for all this time we've been together, why do you think I should?"

Saz was thrown. She'd been expecting an interrogation, demands for truth, fury that Matilda had been put in danger, horror and anger about Carrie. This was not what she'd been frightened of. "I just …"

"You want absolution, Saz."

"I do, yes of course, but I need to tell you …"

210

"Crap. You want me to listen to whatever you have to say and then say it's OK. But I'm not a priest and I'm not a therapist and I know you've been lying to me. I know stuff's been going on, was going on. I've never seen you so relieved as you were the other day when I said I had to go up to Scotland. You wanted me out of the way, it was obvious. And it was really hurtful, but I knew you weren't going to tell me what was happening, because you've never told me all of what's going on with you, and I've ended up just figuring that's what you're like. It's who you are. So I went off and you got on with whatever it was that you needed to do. Ending in this. This fucking mess." Molly was shaking with the effort of keeping her voice down, holding in her anger.

"I need to tell you about it, why it happened …"

"But I don't need to hear it. Whatever has been going on, you want me to listen and hear your story and make it OK for you. It's like me telling everyone I could find about Matilda's birth. And then all the details of my dad's death. The funeral and the wake and all of it. I needed to make those things into stories so I could deal with them. It's what we do, we turn our events into stories so we can handle them."

"Right, and …"

"Shut up, Saz. I'm telling you I don't want to know. I don't want you to tell me a story that's going to make this OK. Carrie is dead. You can't make that OK."

Saz sobbing again, silent now, sobs wrenching her stomach muscles, curling her body in on itself, as if force of wanting could twist her back to Carrie then, not Carrie now.

"I know. I know. And I'm sorry. And it's my fault."

"Did you push the bottle into her neck?"

"No."

"Did that woman—Janine—did she mean to?"

"No … I don't think so."

"Right, so it was an accident. A really bad one."

"But it's my fault she was there, in our flat."

"Yeah. It is. But you didn't kill her."

"She's still dead. She's still fucking dead."

"Yes she is."

"And there are lies, Moll."

Molly groaned, rolled onto her back, eyes scanning the no-vision ceiling. "I expect there are. Have you been having an affair?"

"No."

"Is Matilda OK?"

"Yes … yes she is. You saw her. Don't you think she is?"

"Well, we're probably going to have to pay for a fuck of a lot of therapy later on, but she seems OK just now. There are a whole lot of other questions, Saz, that I don't even want to ask you. You've never told me everything, that's how you are. Hell, maybe it's even something I like about you, not knowing it all." Molly reached out and ran her hands over Saz's thigh, the healed but still jagged skin. "I accepted these burn scars of yours, all that time healing, because I love you. Sure, you told me some of how it happened, but not all of it. You've never talked about all of it. And when you came back from the trip with the band? I knew stuff had happened. Not just the violence, but other things. And I never asked you about that, because I didn't want to know the answer. All I've ever wanted from you is that you be here with me. And now with Matilda and me. That's what I want. You with me."

"I don't know how to be with you without telling you, though … there's things from way back. Stuff about who I was, how I was, when we were kids. Well, not even that young really …"

Molly put her hand on Saz's arm, lightly, definitively. "I'm sorry, but that's your problem, not mine. I've always known that you had stuff you didn't look at, things you were running away from."

"You never said?"

"Why should I? I don't need to know everything, Saz. I don't want to know everything. I don't want to know about the things in your past you want me to forgive. Because it's not my job. Dealing with whatever guilts you have is not my job. I've loved you from pretty much when I first met you—that Saz. That woman." Her hands now moving, to Saz's face, shoulders, arms. "This woman. I still do. If you have things to deal with about your past, then that's yours, not mine. Just like what happened today is yours to deal with, not mine. I can't fix any of it. And anyway, it's not fair of you to ask me to take it on. What if I didn't like what you had to say?"

"How do you mean?"

"What if I let you tell me whatever it is you want to confess, and then I discover I can't love you? Can't bear to be with you?"

"But you do love me …"

"My Saz, that's who I love. Like you love the Molly you know. Your Molly. You might not love me in the hospital, at work. You might not love me when I make decisions about people's lives every day. And sometimes I make the wrong decisions. I've made terrible wrong decisions that really matter. Because I'm human, I fuck up. Sometimes we all fuck up."

"But this is different."

"Maybe. It doesn't matter." Molly reached for Saz's hand in the dark. "Of course it all feels bloody horrible just now, it is bloody horrible. Please don't risk us just because you want me to make you feel better about some crap from your past, and the awful thing that happened today. I can't fix how you feel, you have to do that for yourself."

"What if I can't?"

"Then you can't. And you move on anyway. People do bad things all the time, Saz. Telling me all about it, letting someone else know? That doesn't make the bad go away, it just shares it round. I do love you, but I don't want to share your bad."

"I don't know how to do this, Moll."

"Neither do I. Cry and get on with it. Time doesn't heal, but you do get used to it eventually. At least that's what I'm hoping."

All over, nothing resolved and Carrie still dead. Molly folded herself into Saz's body, talked out and tired. There was a light rain in the wind outside, leaves glistening in the blown damp. Matilda smiled in her dream. Saz barely slept, and in the morning Matilda woke and laughed and cried and Saz and Molly carried on.

Janine Marsden killed herself two nights later on the remand wing of a women's prison. They couldn't get her to a psych unit in time, there just weren't enough beds. She was one of fifteen women who killed themselves in custody that year. The suicide watch that kept her awake by shining a torch in her face every quarter of an hour still gave her another fourteen and a half minutes to cut her veins with the hair clip she'd found wedged into the gap between floor and skirting board. Janine Marsden had no intention of going back to a place of pale green walls.

Saz grieved for Carrie, and most of her grieving she did alone.

Will Gallagher was a tabloid hero. Saved his old friend's life, and that of her child. And even when he admitted some of the story, a little of his own past involvement with Janine Marsden—careful not to name any other names, not to implicate anyone else who'd been involved, honorable mentions only—even when he talked about his less than gentlemanly actions towards her back then, his unfortunate laddish behavior—he sounded OK. He sounded good actually. Someone who'd learned from his mistakes, who'd tried to put it right, wanted to do good. Will Gallagher became the spokesman for an anti-bullying campaign in schools. They made some great ads.

Molly wore the white suit to Carrie's funeral. Saz wore black, and the fucking gorgeous boots. Carrie wore a high-necked pink and orange minidress. She looked amazing.

Stella Duffy has published ten novels. She was long-listed for the 2004 Orange Prize for Fiction for her novel *State of Happiness* which has been optioned by Fiesta Productions and Zentropa, for whom she is also writing the screenplay. Duffy's short story "Martha Grace" won CWA Macallan Short Story Dagger in 2002. Her novels have been published in the USA, Italy, France, Germany, Spain, Brazil, Japan, and Russia.

Stella Duffy was born in London, grew up in Tokoroa, New Zealand, and has lived back in London since 1986. She is married to the writer Shelley Silas.

Bloody Brits Press

BLUE GENES
A Kate Brannigan Mystery

V.L. McDermid

"There is no one in contemporary crime fiction who has managed to combine the visceral and the humane as well as Val McDermid.... She's the best we've got."
—The New York Times Book Review

"Val McDermid is one of the bright lights of the mystery field."
—The Washington Post

Making babies becomes a matter of life and death for Manchester's answer to V.I. Warshawski

Kate Brannigan's having a bad week and she can't even cry on her best friend's shoulder, for Alexis has worries of her own. Her girlfriend Chris is pregnant, and when the doctor responsible for the illegal fertility treatment is murdered, Alexis needs Kate like she's never done before ...

Blue Genes is the fifth Kate Brannigan Mystery.

ISBN 1-932859-23-3 $13.95

Available at your local bookstore
or call toll-free 866-390-7426
or order online at www.bloodybritspress.com